C0-ASR-809

WITHDRAWN

THE SHELL
GAME

THE SHELL GAME

GAME

•

Mona Ingram

AVALON BOOKS

NEW YORK

Published by Thomas Bouregy & Co., Inc.
160 Madison Avenue, New York, NY 10016

Library of Congress Cataloging-in-Publication Data

Ingram, Mona.
  The shell game / Mona Ingram.
      p.   cm.
  ISBN 978-0-8034-9835-8 (acid-free paper)
  I. Title.

  PR9199.4.I54S54 2007
  813'.6—dc22

                          2007003746

PRINTED IN THE UNITED STATES OF AMERICA
ON ACID-FREE PAPER
BY HADDON CRAFTSMEN, BLOOMSBURG, PENNSYLVANIA

For Jack

Prologue

Tuning out the voices around the conference table, Rebecca swiveled her chair toward the window. When had she become bored with market share and demographics? She didn't know. Darting a sideways glance at her writing team, she was thankful to see that they were paying attention to the presentation. Her gaze drifted back to the busy harbor. A seaplane lifted off, water streaming from its floats like a string of crystal beads. Vancouver's harbor was widely thought to be the most beautiful in North America—Rebecca had no argument with that. A Seabus darted out from the terminal, and she leaned forward, watching its progress.

". . . that is, if Rebecca can tear herself away from the window."

Dean Cooper's caustic tone cut through her reverie and she turned to find him glaring at her. It didn't matter, she thought, that she worked twelve to fourteen hours a day when they were shooting the highly rated television series. The producer was relentless when it came to *Hearts On Fire.*

He was right, of course. Lately she'd been easily distracted every time she looked out the window and saw the water. But it wasn't the harbor she saw when she looked through the plate glass. It was a small bay in Ontario's cottage country, dotted with waterlilies and sparkling in the summer sun. The bay where she'd grown up. She regarded Dean calmly, knowing that he wouldn't understand her recent bouts of nostalgia. Until recently, she had been just as driven as the producer. Driven to create better, more compelling scripts. Driven to maintain the show's number-one position. She understood his attitude, but that didn't mean she had to like it.

"Sorry, Dean." She forced her lips into a conciliatory smile. "My mind was somewhere else." She hated to apologize, but if she didn't he'd take his anger out on everyone else at the table. Frank Howell, the show's creator, nodded imperceptibly in her direction, his eyes warm with understanding. One of the few people who appreciated how hard she worked, he never failed to offer a verbal pat on the back when the scripts were submitted. *Hearts On Fire* was a hit, and at Frank's instigation, she'd been offered the position of head writer. He couldn't understand why she'd asked for time to consider it.

"Right, then." Dean pursed his lips, and Rebecca suppressed a shudder of dislike. "I have some exciting news. We've just completed negotiations with Catherine Stuart, who will join the cast next season."

Rebecca couldn't believe what she was hearing. "And when were you going to tell us about this?"

"I'm telling you now."

"But Dean." She fought to control her rising temper. "We have the whole next season plotted out." She glanced at Frank Howell, who suddenly couldn't meet her eyes.

"The storylines are all approved. The shooting schedules . . ." her voice trailed off.

Dean waved his hand dismissively. "Get together with Frank. He can tell you what we have in mind for her character." He paused, looking at her curiously. "I thought you'd be excited."

Rebecca slumped back in her chair. If he didn't understand, then she wasn't about to explain it to him.

Jay Franklin, one of the talented writers, leaned closer. "The guy's an idiot," he murmured. "He has no idea how difficult it's going to be to drop-kick a new character into the mix." He tapped a pencil against the table, and Rebecca could tell he was already thinking about how it could be accomplished.

The door opened, and Dean looked up from his notes, clearly annoyed. "I told you, Cindy. No interruptions."

"It's important," the receptionist said, refusing to back down. Her eyes, filled with tears, came to rest on Rebecca.

"Well, don't just stand there. What is it?"

An icy chill crept down Rebecca's spine and she rose from her chair, ignoring the producer. Making her way around the conference table, she drew the receptionist out into the hall, closing the door behind her. "Cindy, what's the matter?" she asked, although deep inside she already knew the answer. The floor seemed to tilt under her feet, and she moved toward the reception desk as though in a dream. White-knuckled hands clutched the edge of the desk, and it took her a moment to realize that they belonged to her.

"I'm sorry, Rebecca." Cindy was making a valiant effort not to cry. "Your grandmother's doctor phoned." She walked toward the reception desk. "He left his number for you to call him as soon as possible."

Rebecca stared at the message slip. "She's dead, isn't she?" She didn't recognize her own voice.

Cindy's mouth quivered. "And I know how much you were looking forward to spending time with her this summer." She darted back behind the massive reception desk. "I'm so sorry, Rebecca."

"Thanks." She looked back down at the message, but it hadn't changed. Somehow, her legs carried her back to her office. Standing in front of the window, she was transported back to Water Lily Bay. For a brief moment, she thought she could smell the sweet scent of pine trees. The sensation was so real, she had to steady herself against the window frame. She hadn't been back once during the summer since she left all those years ago. Back to the town where she'd spent the happiest days of her life—and one memorable night that changed her life forever.

Chapter 1

Rebecca brought the car to a halt at the top of the driveway. Just under twenty-eight hundred miles from Vancouver. Determined to arrive in time for the funeral, she'd left within hours and driven straight through, stopping only twice to catch a few hours of sleep. No wonder she was exhausted. The dull pain of regret that had been her unwelcome companion during the long trip started to drain away and she took a deep breath, savoring the evocative smells of the early-summer evening. Vancouver's tangy sea air was all well and good, but this was home. The resinous scent of the pine trees was sweeter than any perfume, and she berated herself for never coming back to visit in the summer.

Gran had always stopped at this precise spot, turning off the car's motor before coasting down to the lodge in splendid silence. She smiled softly in remembrance. Those had been happy times.

"This one's for you, Gran." The car rolled down the hill, the sound muffled by a layer of pine needles. The old building came into view, bathed in that magical golden

light she recalled so well from her childhood. Tucked
back into the trees, Water Lily Bay Lodge commanded a
spectacular view of Lake Joseph, befitting its status as
grande dame of the lake.

She stepped out of the car and stretched, massaging the
small of her back. Her gaze swept out over the water, her
chest tightening as poignant memories wrapped around
her heart. There wasn't a breath of air moving on the lake,
and, as though drawn by a magnet, she found herself
standing on the shore.

The water lapped against the bottom of the dock and
she blinked rapidly, fighting the tears that welled up in her
eyes. Odd, wasn't it, how simple sounds could unleash
such strong emotion. Cocking her head to one side, she
wondered if her imagination was playing tricks on her.
She walked slowly to the end of the dock. No, that was
definitely the sound of someone swimming. She shuddered, recalling only too well how the waters remained
chilly until well into July.

Shading her eyes, she squinted in the direction of the
swimmer. Muscular arms flashed as they cut through the
silvery water. Strong legs propelled the swimmer in a
smooth, powerful crawl that could only be mastered with
years of practice. She stood mesmerized as he
approached the ladder. With one fluid movement, the man
was on the dock, water streaming down his body.

Rebecca inhaled sharply and stepped back. His face
was shadowed, but in the slanting light, the muscles in his
shoulders and arms were clearly defined. A broad torso
tapered down to slim hips and her throat went dry as he
slicked his hair back with both hands. Her eyes flickered
over his bathing suit and continued down the muscular
legs.

He flashed her a heart-stopping grin as he bent over to

pick up a towel from the Adirondack chairs at the end of the dock. "Hello Becky. Good to see you." He slung the towel around his neck and stepping forward, he extended his hand. "I'm sorry about Stella. Your grandmother was one of a kind."

Her hand found its way into his. His voice was deeper, but she would have recognized it anywhere, even though it had been . . . what was it? Eleven years? Her fingers burned against his cool skin and she yanked back her hand. Her lips parted, but no sound came out. Eyes that were somewhere between slate grey and dark blue peered at her with startling intensity, as though trying to read her thoughts. She bristled angrily. It wasn't fair—he had no right to affect her like this after so much time had passed. She tossed back her hair, fighting for composure.

"What are you doing here?" It came out as a croak.

"Having an evening swim. I would have waited for you, but I didn't know you'd be arriving tonight." The eyes flashed in amusement.

"That's not what I mean, and you know it." She swung her arm to encompass the bay. "What are you doing here, on Gran's property?"

He grinned lazily, and she flushed as his eyes held hers. "And here I thought you weren't glad to see me."

"Mitchell Burton, stop talking nonsense and tell me what you're doing here." She stamped her foot impatiently.

Without appearing to move, he closed the distance between them and grasped her arm. His face hovered close to hers, and for a moment she thought she saw desire lurking behind those incredible eyes. "Careful Becks, you almost stepped off the dock."

She looked behind her. He was right, she had almost gone for an early dip in the lake. Her skin tingled from his touch, and she covered her reaction with a short laugh. "I guess I'm tired. It's been a long drive. But you still haven't answered me."

His eyes scanned the shoreline, and she saw in them the same affection she felt for the property. "I live here."

This time her mouth dropped all the way open. "What?" She looked from the beautiful old building back to him. "You live here at the lodge?"

"No. Not the lodge." He started to walk along the dock, and Becky followed him. "I live in the boathouse."

"In the boathouse?"

"I think I hear an echo." He grinned down at her. "Yes, I live in the boathouse."

"But . . ." Her mind raced. "There's nowhere to live in there." The building in question was visible through the trees. She'd inquired about the new siding a few years ago and Gran had told her that she'd hired a handyman to put it up.

"There is, actually. I made the loft into an apartment, and I work downstairs." They continued along the dock, walking side by side.

Becky peered at the old building. "What does that say?" A small sign was affixed to the wall by the side door.

"It says *Custom Boats*." Mitch tapped his chest. "That's me."

"Gran said she had someone helping her with the place." Her eyes widened. "Don't tell me . . ."

"Don't tell you what? That I helped your grandmother when she needed it?" He gave her a sharp look. "Somebody had to. Besides which, I'm perfectly capable, or so I'm told."

Rebecca spun around to face him. "That was a low blow, Mitch Burton. Anyway, what do you know about being there for someone?" She waved a hand in front of her face. "Don't get me started. I'm too tired to get into that right now."

For a brief heartbeat, Rebecca thought she saw a flash of pain on his face, then his demeanor changed abruptly. "Suit yourself. I'll get the key to the lodge and help you with your bags."

Her eyes followed him as he walked along the well-worn path to the boathouse. Why was she surprised that he had turned into such a handsome man? Even in high school she'd been aware of his dark good looks. But that was many years ago, and she'd put him firmly out of her mind.

Or had she? With a high-pressure career in the television industry, she didn't have time to dwell on old, forgotten dreams. "So what if he's here?" she asked out loud. "It was just a high school crush." Then why had her spirits lifted at the sound of his voice? She leaned against the side of her car, fighting the memories that threatened to overwhelm her. She hadn't expected to see him here— or anywhere for that matter. As to his tenancy in the boathouse, she couldn't bear to have him that close. She hadn't had time to consider her legal position. Getting through the funeral was her top priority. After that she would see the lawyer and terminate Mitch's rental agreement as soon as possible.

"Let me help you with that."

His reappearance startled her, and she winced at his impersonal tone. Gone was the gently teasing way he'd greeted her. She pointed to her largest suitcase. "I'll just take that one for tonight. It has everything I need."

He nodded, lifting the suitcase as though it weighed nothing. It was too late to take back those hurtful remarks, and she watched him silently as he went up the stairs, muscles firm under a white T-shirt.

She eased Pekoe out of his carrier. The orange tabby cat dug in his claws, wary eyes darting around the unfamiliar territory.

Mitch came back down and leaned into the trunk. "I might as well haul all your stuff up tonight." Spotting the cat, he raised his hand as though to soothe him, then dropped it just as quickly. With a quick shake of his head, he picked up the two remaining suitcases and ran up the stairs.

Rebecca followed and stood blinking in the light of the mudroom. "Thank you." Raking her fingers nervously through the cat's fur, she studied him through the screen door. He stood on the landing under a pool of yellow light. His hair, still wet from the lake, glistened darkly. Her eyes flickered over his square jaw, then lingered on his full lips. He was the same, but so much more!

He looked back at her. He seemed to be sizing her up, as though she were a stranger. *"In many ways I am a stranger,"* she thought sadly, trying to read his thoughts. Whatever was between us disappeared on a hot summer night much like this one. But his eyes still had the ability to mesmerize her, and she stood in the doorway, skewered by his gaze. The cat squirmed in her arms, asking to be set down.

He shook his head, as though coming out of a trance. "We'll have to talk eventually, you know." He looked at her evenly. "Let me know when you're ready." With a curt nod, he disappeared down the stairs.

Becky stared after him. Walking closer to the door, she placed her palm on the screen, peering out into the black night. Moments later a light came on, barely visible through the trees. Having Mitch this close was unsettling, yet at the same time she was comforted knowing that he was nearby. She turned back into the familiar old home and made her way into the kitchen. A bouquet of wild-flowers sat in the center of the scarred wooden table. A note was propped up against it. *I've put a few things in the fridge for your first night. Welcome home. Mitch.*

She slumped onto a kitchen chair and held her head in her hands. Why did he have to be so considerate? It was just like him. Her shoulders shook, and she didn't know if she was laughing or crying, but she was in no mood to analyze her own feelings. Especially with Mitch Burton nearby.

Mitch switched on the overhead light and stood just inside the door, staring blankly at the upturned hull. His mind was reeling. Becky had changed in so many ways he didn't know what to think. The gentle, sensitive girl he'd known in school had changed into an ill-tempered, uptight woman. Okay, he thought reluctantly, she was also gorgeous. Walking alongside the hull, he ran his hand over the surface, admiring the sleek lines of the runabout that was his current project. The shed smelled sweetly of old wood, shavings, and the stains and finishes he used as part of his craft. The corner of his mouth slid sideways into a reluctant grin. Those familiar everyday smells couldn't replace the memory of her perfume. It had invaded his senses when he'd caught her as she was about to fall into the water. Maybe he should have let her fall. But he doubted that even a dunk in the chilly water would temper the anger that sizzled so near the surface. He shook his head sadly and gazed around his workshop. It had been his haven for several years now, and for the first time in his adult life, he was content. Unlike his jobs in the 'real world', he could gauge his daily progress by what he accomplished with his hands. Working with mostly recycled woods, he felt a pride of craftsmanship that was more valuable than any monetary reward. He was finally doing something he loved and being back in Muskoka was the icing on the cake.

His mind wandered back to Becky. She'd had every right to be disappointed in him all those years ago. The idea of meeting her again had filled him with nervous anticipation, as well as dread. He'd thought he was prepared for any reaction, but he'd been completely thrown off guard by her open hostility. After all, she'd never made any attempt to contact him. He'd always assumed that she had decided to get on with her life. It was still painful, much as he hated to admit it.

Leaning over his worktable, he stared at the boat plans spread out before him, but he couldn't concentrate. He wandered out to his small deck and sank down into a chair.

When he'd pulled himself up onto the dock after his swim and saw her standing there, the old sparks seemed to flicker and ignite. For a brief moment he'd seen approval in those flashing eyes, and then it had disappeared. When she'd almost stepped backward into the water, he'd been reminded of the clumsy teenager she'd once been. Perhaps a shadow of that remained, but the woman that had emerged took his breath away. Her auburn hair hadn't changed much; it was still a riot of curls and his fingers tensed as he envisioned how it had looked tonight on the dock, shining in the last golden rays of the sun. Her hazel eyes hadn't lost their power to make his heart race, and he suddenly wished he knew what had caused her to change so dramatically, for change she had. With a lingering look at the boat, he climbed the stairs to the loft. If today had been bad, tomorrow would be even worse. He was dreading it already.

Rebecca shot out of bed as the strident sound of the telephone broke through the fog of sleep. Pekoe raised his head from the foot of the bed, golden eyes alert to the new sound.

"All right, all right, I'm coming." She picked up the old-fashioned instrument, taking a deep breath to steady herself. "Hello?"

"Miss Lambert?" The man's voice was crisp. "Wade Furness here." He paused. "I hope I didn't wake you. I expected to hear from you yesterday."

Becky fumbled to find her watch. "The drive took a bit longer than I thought, but I'm here now."

"I'd like to offer my condolences about your grandmother."

Rebecca sat down on the edge of the bed. "Thank you."

"I'm sorry to bother you today, with the funeral and all, but I'm leaving on holiday this weekend and I was hoping you could come to my office this afternoon." He paused. "After the funeral, of course."

Becky found herself nodding as she slipped her feet into her slippers. He had told her before she left Vancouver that he was leaving. "Yes, of course. What time would be good for you?"

"Can you come around four? I have freed up some time for you then. Your grandmother's will was straightforward, so it shouldn't take too long."

"All right, thanks. See you then." She padded into the kitchen and made herself a cup of coffee. With Pekoe rubbing up against her leg, she set out a dish of water and food. Coffee mug in hand, she sauntered out to the screened porch and settled into her favorite wicker chair.

A slight breeze set the water lapping against the shore. It was a peaceful sound. The whole bay was peaceful. As a young bride, Stella had come to this area for summer holidays, eventually making it her permanent home. She had often spoken of her love for the property and how it had seemed only natural to bring Rebecca here to live after her parents were drowned on the Great Lakes when she was very young.

Her heart twisted as she thought of her beloved grandmother. Stella had been delighted when Rebecca made her annual visit this past Christmas, announcing her plans to spend time at the lodge this summer. She was aging noticeably, and Rebecca had been looking forward to the visit. But in spite of her good intentions, she'd been too late. It hadn't quite sunk in yet.

She got up and stretched, wandering idly around the great room. Running across most of the front of the lodge, it was a favorite of the Bed & Breakfast customers who returned year after year. Informal clusters of easy chairs dotted the room, and a semi-circular grouping in front of the fireplace encouraged guests to mingle.

Stella had turned the lodge into a B&B after Rebecca moved to British Columbia. She had limited the number of rental rooms to six, and over the years had developed a loyal clientele, mostly seniors. "I only do it for the company," she would say with a laugh. "I certainly don't need the money." Rebecca smiled sadly at the memory. It was true. Gran had needed the company more than the money. Even so, the Bed & Breakfast brought in a healthy income.

Sunlight danced on the lake, sending flashes of light

dancing through the pines. The two Adirondack chairs at the end of the dock sat like silent sentinels, and once more Becky felt the strong pull of the Muskokas. An idyllic setting for her formative years, she had nothing but happy memories of her early life here. Her gaze drifted to the boathouse and her breath caught in her throat. Well . . . mostly happy.

During the funeral, Rebecca had forced herself to concentrate on the colored patch of sunlight on the floor. She knew every color variation in the stained-glass windows that ran along the side of the church. When she was young, she'd snuggle up beside her grandmother and watch the colors creep across the floor, making up stories to pass the time.

The church had been full, the doors in the back open for those who'd arrived too late. They stood respectfully, listening to the short service. The rest had been a blur. The reception laid on by the ladies' guild of the church, the countless hands to shake, and the murmured words of sympathy.

She tore off her dark clothes and slipped into a pair of cool white slacks topped with an emerald green blouse. Her watch told her she had twenty minutes to get back downtown.

The lawyer's office was in a newer building on a side street in town. Becky pulled up in front, beside a vintage Harley. With an appreciative glance at the old machine, she entered the building.

"Miss Lambert?" The receptionist greeted her pleasantly. "Mr. Furness is waiting for you. This way please."

At the end of the hall, she opened a door and ushered Becky inside. Wade Furness stood up and extended his hand. Becky moved toward him, and then froze in her steps. "What are you doing here?"

Mitch stood up as she entered, unfolding his long frame from one of the chairs in front of the lawyer's desk. "I don't know." He looked at her cautiously. "Wade asked me to wait until you arrived." He sat down again. He wore jeans that fit him so well they should be against the law. His shirt was faded chambray, crisply ironed. She tore her eyes away from him and turned to the lawyer. "What is he doing here?"

"Please sit down, Miss Lambert." He shuffled some papers in a file and linked his fingers, waiting for her to get settled.

"Stella Grant was my client for over twenty years, and I would like to say that I respected her very much." He peered over half-glasses at Becky, then his gaze shifted to Mitch. "When she asked me to prepare her will, she was of sound mind." A small smile flirted with the corners of his mouth. "She went so far as to ask her doctor for written confirmation of that fact, although no one who knew her at the time ever doubted it." He lifted a sheaf of papers and then dropped them. "Let's get to the point. She has divided everything equally between the two of you. She has named you joint executors." He sat back in his chair.

Mitch leaned forward. "You can't be serious. Why would she do that? I'm no relation to her." He glanced at Becky and then back to the lawyer. "This is ridiculous."

"Nevertheless, those were her wishes." He steepled his fingers. "She told me that's what you would say. It sounds like she knew you well."

"But . . ." He spread his hands. "This doesn't make any sense."

Rebecca's brow furrowed as she watched Mitch's reaction. He seemed genuinely surprised. As a matter of fact, for a moment back there he had the look of someone who was trapped.

"Listen." Mitch leaned forward, tapping a long finger on the desk. The whole scene was unreal, and Becky focused on his hand, thinking how strong and competent it looked. "Before this goes any farther, I'd like you to draw up some papers relinquishing anything Stella left to me and turning it over to Becky." He glanced at her, his eyes almost desperate. "It should all be hers."

The lawyer shook his head slowly. "Hold on now. You'll both be getting copies of everything, but Stella specifically asked me to read a few items while you were here together. So if you'll allow me, I'll proceed." He looked at each of them in turn. "These are her words. She insisted on that." He rustled the papers.

I have given a great deal of thought to the disposition of my assets, and I want you both to accept my decision. I've never had much use for those fancy wills, so what I'm asking of you is not legally binding, but these are my most heartfelt wishes.

First of all, I'd like you both to take my ashes, along with Hugh's, and scatter them on the beach somewhere in Bermuda. It's important that you do this together, and I'd like it done as soon as possible after my death.

My second request is that you not sell the property, either to each other or to a third party, for at least one year after my death. I know from experience that decisions made in haste can lead to years of regret.

My third and last request may be the most difficult. There are many customers of Water Lily Bay Lodge

*who look upon it as their home away from home for
a few days every summer. I'd like to ask you to honor
any reservations I have accepted, at least for the first
year after my death. After that time, you may do as
you wish.*

Wade Furness removed his glasses and peered at the
woman and the man across the desk. "Stella told me that
you have joint signing authority on her account."

"You're saying that either one of us can write checks
on her account?" Becky's face reflected her disbelief.

Mitch groaned and sank back in his chair. "She said she
wanted me to have signing authority on her checking
account in case she became incapacitated. I resisted at
first, but she could be very persuasive."

"She knew you were reluctant." The lawyer looked at
him appraisingly. "But she trusted you. That was what
mattered."

Mitch shook his head. "I'll say this for her, she was a
crafty one."

The lawyer dug through the papers and extracted a
computer printout. "She also transferred the property. You
own it jointly now."

"This is too much." Rebecca's voice shook.

"Listen Becky, I'm sorry. I didn't know what she was
doing." The chill that had been in his voice last night had
been replaced by confusion.

She smiled briefly at him, a glimmer of her old self
before the pinched look returned. "I'm not concerned
about the money." She fluttered her hands. "The estate
isn't what's bothering me; it's all these conditions." She
laughed, but it was a mirthless sound. "I'm beginning to
think that I didn't know Gran very well."

"No kidding." Mitch stood up and accepted the large

envelope from the lawyer before extending his hand. "Thanks, I guess." His grin was wry. "This has been quite a shock."

Becky tucked her envelope under her arm and shook hands with the lawyer. "When will you return from your holiday?" She motioned to include Mitch. "In case we need to ask you any questions, I mean."

"I'll be gone for three weeks. My receptionist can give you the precise dates." He looked at them speculatively. "I can only tell you that Stella didn't ask these things of you lightly. She knew she was asking a lot."

Mitch looked at the envelope in his hand as though it contained nuclear waste. "You can say that again."

Becky nodded her head in agreement. "It's a lot to absorb."

"Good luck, then." The lawyer walked them to the front door, and they were suddenly out in the bright sunshine.

She looked up at him, shading her eyes from the sun. "I didn't see you at the funeral."

His eyes flared. "I was there. Listen, do you want to go somewhere and have a coffee?" He waved the brown envelope in the air. "Talk things over?" He had regained his composure and she resented him for it.

"Hardly." She cringed inwardly as she realized how rude she sounded, but she couldn't help herself. His presence unnerved her, and apart from the shock of the estate, she knew she would blurt out something even worse if she went with him. "I think I'll wander along Main Street and see what's new."

"Suit yourself." The smile left his face, and he approached the Harley, shoving the envelope into the saddlebags before climbing on. His long legs reached the ground on either side of the beautiful machine, and Becky's breath caught in her throat as she looked at him, poised to take off. His hands caressed the grips on the handlebars, and for a moment she allowed herself to remember the way they used to walk together, fingers linked. His eyes glittered, as though reading her thoughts.

"You've changed, Becky." He kicked the starter and the rumble was visceral. "See you later," he mouthed, over the noise of the motorcycle.

Her eyes followed him as he backed out and drove to the corner. Then he turned toward the lake and disappeared. She realized that she had been holding her breath and let it out through pursed lips. Mitch Burton was dangerous; unless she went against her grandmother's wishes, she would have to deal with him for the next year. The prospect had a certain appeal, she admitted reluctantly, sliding behind the wheel. Then the memories washed over her like a cold rain, and she chided herself harshly. How could she forget, even for a moment, how he had hurt her?

"Rebecca Lambert, is that you?" The door to the flower shop flew open and a slim woman stood with one hand on the doorframe. "You look fantastic."

Becky gaped at the attractive woman. "Penny? My gosh, you've lost so much weight I didn't recognize you at first."

The other woman blushed, and a shy smile transformed the familiar face. "Thanks. It was hard work, but I finally did it." Her face sobered. "Sorry about your grandmother. Stella was an amazing woman."

"You have no idea." Becky couldn't resist the wry response. "Although I wish I'd spent more time with her these past few years. Looking back on it, yearly Christmas visits weren't enough."

"Listen. Do you have time for coffee? I have one of the students in for work experience, and things are quiet right now, so I could get away." She indicated the coffee shop across the road.

"I'd like that." The two women were soon settled in one of the comfortable booths.

"Have you worked at the flower shop for long?" Becky glanced across the street. "It looks much the same. A bit nicer, perhaps."

"Why thank you. I've owned it for the past five years."

"Congratulations!" Becky's enthusiasm was genuine. "Are you enjoying it?"

"Most of the time. I can't really think of anything I'd rather do." She leaned forward eagerly. "I hope you don't mind if I gush a bit, but *Hearts On Fire* is one of my favorite TV programs. Imagine, you being a famous writer." She signaled for two coffees. "Your grandmother was so proud of you."

A shadow flickered across Rebecca's eyes. "I thought there'd be more time . . . you know?"

"If it's any consolation, she was over the moon that you were coming for a visit this summer. That should count for something."

"I suppose so." Rebecca spotted a wedding band on her friend's hand. "So you're married now. Anyone I know?"

"I don't think so. Andy came to town a few years after you left. What about you? You left so abruptly. I often wondered what happened to you."

Rebecca's gaze wandered over the stores lining the street, many of them the same as when she left. "Gran was adamant that I get what she called 'a proper education.' She sent me away from everything that was familiar, and that was hard." She shrugged her shoulders. "It took me a while to get over being mad at her, but eventually I cooled down and started to make friends. As usual, she was right. That education led to my career as a writer." She smiled at her friend. "So tell me about the town. What's new?"

Penny shrugged. "It's still much the same as when we were growing up. Of course property values have sky-rocketed since we became 'cottage country'. There's even a new housing subdivision where the old trailer park used to be." She signaled for a refill on their coffee. "Speaking of the trailer park, Mitch Burton left about the same time you did, and he was gone for ages." She paused reflec-tively while the waitress refilled their mugs. "I always thought you and Mitch would end up together. You two used to be inseparable."

Rebecca stirred her coffee, unwilling to meet her friend's eyes. "That was just high school stuff."

Penny nodded. "When I bought the flower shop from Mrs. Jenkins, she told me the most interesting story about Mitch." She acknowledged a greeting through the window and missed the flare of interest on Rebecca's face. "It seems that Mitch ordered a corsage for our graduation dance but he never picked it up. Then a few months later he showed up and paid for it. Interesting, huh?"

Rebecca picked up her mug and blew on the hot coffee, needing a few moments to absorb the information. "Yes, it is."

"Of course he's showed his true colors in the past few years. When the town decided to start a youth outreach program, he was among the first to volunteer. He has an amazing rapport with those troubled young kids. They really look up to him." She gazed into the distance. "Funny how things work out, isn't it?"

Rebecca nodded slowly as she digested this new infor-mation. "It sure is."

Chapter 2

Rebecca's thoughts drifted as she rounded the lake. She had never considered the dollar value of her grandmother's estate. That must be why splitting it didn't really bother her. But why Mitch, of all people? Her lips curled in a reluctant smile. Gran was probably enjoying all this from her safe perch somewhere up in heaven.

Cresting a rise, she peered eagerly through the trees. That first glimpse of sun-sparkled water had always meant she was close to home. As she passed a series of long, shady driveways punctuated by listing mailboxes, she was comforted by a sense of belonging. Every twist in the road brought her closer to the lodge.

She coasted to a stop beside the back entrance. The whine of a saw broke the silence, an unnecessary reminder of Mitch's presence at the boathouse. He'd been in her thoughts all the way home, and she recalled the way his smile had disappeared outside the lawyer's office. Was it any wonder, considering the churlish way she'd spoken to him? Setting the grocery bags on the kitchen table, her eyes fell on the bouquet of wildflowers he'd left for her.

It was time to swallow her pride and ask for a truce. Fearing that she would change her mind, she rushed into her bedroom and quickly pulled a brush through her hair, then changed into a pair of shorts and a T-shirt. Grabbing a couple of cans of iced tea, she headed down the stairs and ran lightly along the path to the boathouse.

Her steps slowed as she reached the building. The doors stood open, and a radio played softly in the background. Mitch had his back to her; he was bent over an upturned hull, sanding with long, fluid strokes. Sawdust speckled his forearms and dusted his dark hair. Finer particles hung suspended in the air, a hazy yellow mist in the slanting sun. His movements were almost sensual, and her breath caught in her throat as she watched him straighten and then run his palm along the wood he had just sanded. Nodding his head in satisfaction, he lowered it to sight along the surface then stilled, sensing her presence. With one hand resting casually on the hull, he turned, and she heard his sharp intake of breath as his eyes raked over her bare legs and continued slowly up her body before meeting her eyes.

"What do you want?" His voice was tight, but at least he hadn't asked her to leave.

She held up the cans, the invitation clear. "I was wondering if you'd like a break. If you're still speaking to me, that is."

He studied her, and for a moment she wondered if he was going to refuse her invitation. "That sounds like a good idea. Give me a couple of minutes, and I'll get rid of some of this sawdust." He indicated two deck chairs on the worn planks outside the boathouse and disappeared inside.

Rebecca was glad to sit down. She hadn't felt this nervous since . . . well, she couldn't remember when. She took a deep breath and tried to calm her nerves. Fidgeting nervously, she realized that she had no idea what she wanted to say. In school they'd practically been able to read each other's minds, but this new Mitch was formidable. He was her partner now—for a year at least, and it was time to stop sniping at him. She owed that much to Gran.

Taking a deep, calming breath she looked around, assessing the changes to the boathouse. The old structure looked surprisingly robust, and a new dock extended out into the water, partially shaded by the long silvered leaves of a willow. A sleek mahogany runabout sat alongside, brightwork sparkling in the dappled sunlight. The rich wood gleamed through many coats of finish, a breathtaking reminder of the golden days when wooden boats were plentiful in the waters of Muskoka.

She knew he was behind her before the old plank squealed in protest at his weight. They had always been attuned to each other's moods and movements. In those days of innocence, it had been comfortable. In the intervening years, she had never again been brave enough to open her soul to another person, as she had with Mitch. Nowadays, when a man tried to get close, it was far easier to move on, to claim the pressures of work as an excuse to terminate the relationship. That way, she was assured of not being hurt again. And it worked. She might sometimes miss having a man to call on, but on the other hand she didn't have to worry that he would leave her.

He turned his chair so that it faced hers. "It occurs to me that I don't know what you're thinking any more, Becky. We used to know each other so well." He looked at her with a touch of sadness, then lifted the can to his lips. Leaning back in the chair he stretched out his long legs.

"I still haven't figured out what happened today." He held up a hand. "Let me rephrase that. I know what happened, but I don't know why it happened." He leaned forward, resting his elbows on his knees. "I had no idea what she was up to. If I had, I can assure you I would have tried to talk her out of it. It's important to me that you know that." He waited for her reaction.

"I never doubted you on that score, Mitch. I don't pretend to know Gran's thought process, but I suspect that by leaving you half of her estate she was thanking you for all your help."

"I didn't do all that much. I took her to her doctors' appointments and helped her with her groceries." His mouth twitched. "She never lost her sense of humor. We had a lot of laughs."

"I wish I'd been here for her." Her voice was raw with regret.

"It meant a lot to her that you were going to visit this summer. In the meantime, she loved getting your letters and hearing about what you were doing. I was simply filling in for you. I didn't expect anything like this."

"She really did a number on us, didn't she?"

"Are you upset about that?" He eyed her warily.

"I'm still too exhausted to be upset." And too confused, but her pride wouldn't let her admit it. "Anyway, I learned when I was young not to waste too much time being mad at Gran."

He frowned. "I don't recall you ever being mad at her."

"It was after . . ." she paused and took a deep breath. "It was after high school. I resented the fact that she sent me to college, away from everything I knew. It took a while for me to realize that she was simply doing what she thought was good for me."

"I get the distinct feeling she's still trying to run your

life." A rueful smile lifted the corner of his mouth. "As well as mine. And yet, somehow I can't find it in my heart to be angry with her."

Rebecca permitted her eyes to roam slowly over his face. Each time she looked at him, his appeal was stronger, seeming to reach out and pull her toward him.

"Can I ask you something? Why were you so quick to offer to give up your half of Gran's estate?" A sudden thought chilled her but she had to know. "Did you find the idea of spending time with me so unappealing?" Tears began to burn behind her eyes and she stood up abruptly, turning her back to him. "I'm sorry. I had no right to ask you that."

"You have every right to ask me that, and believe me, that's definitely not the reason." His voice gentled. "It's hard to put into words how I felt this afternoon, but I'll try."

She turned back. "I wish you would."

"My first reaction was of being trapped. It was like I'd suddenly been drawn into something and couldn't find my way out."

"I knew that's how you were feeling!" She blurted it out without thinking.

"Well, whaddya know?" He looked at her appraisingly. "For a while there I thought the Becky I used to know had disappeared." He jiggled the can and then drained it. "But seriously, Becks, I felt as though I were being manipulated." His eyes narrowed. "And if there's anything I detest, it's someone trying to manipulate me." He glanced at her sideways. "I had enough of that in my marriage, thank you very much."

"You were married?" Becky felt her mouth drop open. "I didn't know that."

His gaze wandered out over the water, growing distant

as he put his thoughts into words. "It was while I was living in Toronto. It wasn't until after we were married that I discovered she wanted to make me over into the man of her dreams." He gave a short, dry laugh. "I wish she'd kept looking for Mr. Perfect and left me alone, but no, she was determined. In the beginning we were good together, but as time went on . . ." He scrubbed his face with the palm of his hand. "One good thing came out of the marriage, though. I have a son. She makes my life miserable about seeing him, but I refuse to give up one hour of time with him." He stared into the empty can, lost in thought.

"What's his name?"

"Scott. At least we agreed on that. He's eight now, and growing like the proverbial weed." He shrugged. "She remarried, but that didn't last either. They were divorced last year."

Rebecca topped up her glass and filled his. "All the more reason why you shouldn't give up your half."

"What do you mean?"

"Scott. Even if you don't want the proceeds from Gran's estate you could set it aside for him."

For a moment she thought she saw a flicker of amusement in his eyes. "I'm not exactly broke." He gestured into the boathouse. "As you can see, I have a thriving business." She couldn't tell if he was kidding or not. "After all, how much money does one man need?"

"Mitch Burton, you're exasperating!" Her smile belied her words.

"Look who's talking. You realize, of course, that your reaction to all of this is quite unusual."

"In what way?" She inched forward on her chair.

"Well, let's see. Most people I know would have been outraged to have their inheritance cut in half. But here you are, encouraging me to keep it." He spread his hands. "What's the matter, do you have an allergy to money or something?"

"I could say the same thing to you," she challenged. "At least I haven't talked about giving it up."

"Touché." Suddenly serious, his eyes held her captive. "You're beautiful when you smile, Becky. I hope there's someone in your life who tells you that a lot."

His gentle words chased any clever rejoinders from her head. "Oh, I'll bet you say that to all the girls."

"No," he replied evenly, "I don't." He sat patiently while she composed herself.

"My job keeps me too busy to get involved with anyone." Her voice wavered. "And look where it's got me." She swept her arm in a broad gesture, encompassing the lake and the lodge. "I decide to visit Gran in the summer, but I'm too late." A tear rolled down her cheek and she ignored it. "But this wasn't supposed to be about me. I never could stick to the point." She hiked up her chin and looked him in the eye. "None of that justifies my rude behavior. No matter what happened between us in the past, I shouldn't have spoken to you the way I did. I'd like to apologize."

He leaned forward and picked up her hand. "It's all forgotten. I have just one question for you."

She looked up at him, her brow furrowed. "And that is?"

"Why Bermuda?"

Rebecca stared at him for an instant and then laughed out loud. It felt good. "Isn't she something else? There is a reason, though. Gran and Grandpa had planned to go to Bermuda on their twenty-fifth anniversary, but he died unexpectedly just a few months before." She tilted her head, tuning in to vague memories that lurked in the back of her mind. "You know, she mentioned Bermuda a few times, but I didn't realize it was that important to her. I could have taken her."

"Ah, but it wouldn't have been the same, would it?" He tipped his chair back, a distant smile on his face. "This is better because in a way they'll be going together." He nodded to himself. "And so will we. Be going together, that is."

"So it seems." Her thoughts drifted. "I wish I'd known my grandfather, but maybe it's not too late. While I'm going through Gran's papers, I'll keep my eyes open for old family records. Perhaps some family history will help us understand why she left us with this dilemma."

A gentle breeze rippled the surface of the lake, and she slapped at a mosquito on her leg. "Time to go in," she said reluctantly. "Want to wander along the shore?" They walked side by side in comfortable silence. Pausing by the dock, she looked up at him, an unspoken question in her eyes. He nodded, and they stepped onto the dock in unison, heading toward the end. She couldn't begin to count the number of times they had watched the sunset together when they were young. She was startled out of her reverie when he spoke.

"Do you think she's trying to play Cupid with us?" He didn't seem angry. He seemed curious, and his voice held a hint of amusement.

Rebecca turned away, pretending to study the setting sun. She'd had the same thought . . . several times.

"What makes you think she'd do that?" she murmured.

"I don't know, but I have a feeling she's up to something." The sun slipped below the hills, painting the scattered clouds with a soft pink glow. He placed his hands lightly on her shoulders and turned her around. "After all, she's made sure we have to spend time together." His eyes teased her. "Will that be so difficult?"

Rebecca wasn't sure if she could form a coherent thought. Her skin tingled all over from the brief touch. "I suppose not," she whispered, wishing he would touch her again.

"Where do we go from here?" His voice was deceptively light.

"I'm not sure." In truth, she would like to turn back the clock, but she gave her head a mental shake. These irrational thoughts would have to stop. Besides, this was temporary. She belonged in Vancouver, immersed in her exciting, demanding career. Her breath caught in her throat. Then why did it feel so right being back here?

"Becky." His voice came from far away. "Are you okay?"

"I'm fine," she said, but even to her own ears, she wasn't very convincing.

The concern in his eyes was evident. "You're tired, aren't you? Come on, I'll walk you up to the lodge."

They sauntered up the lawn in the gathering dusk, lost in their own thoughts. He paused at the foot of the stairs, studying her openly. His gaze drifted over her tousled hair, holding her eyes for a moment before moving on to her mouth. He swallowed. "What do you think we should do next? About the estate, I mean. I'll be happy to help you out in any way I can, but I suspect you'd like to be in charge." He grinned. "Just like old times."

"Mitch Burton, that's not true!" Too late, she realized that he was teasing her. "You haven't changed all that much, have you?"

He reached out and ran the back of his fingers down her cheek. "No. I still like the same things." He gazed at her tenderly, and she grabbed at the railing as her knees threatened to buckle.

She was surprised that her voice sounded so normal. "I

think the first thing we should do is check out the bank account."

"You don't need me for that, do you?"

"I guess not. I could do it tomorrow. Let's wait until we get a handle on that before we make any decisions."

"Good idea." He glanced at his watch. "I'd better be on my way. I have a meeting in town. Will I see you tomorrow?"

"I'll come and tell you what I find out." She made shooing motions with her hands. "Get on with you now. I still have to unpack."

She trudged up the stairs, suddenly very tired. Pekoe was nowhere to be seen and it was only after ten minutes of searching that she found the frightened animal cowering under the skirts of an easy chair. "It's okay," she soothed. "I'll take care of you." Her words echoed in her ears as she settled into an overstuffed chair. In the end it was Mitch who had taken care of her grandmother. The cat curled into her lap and she stroked him absently, lost in thought. Not many men would display the caring and compassion necessary to help an old woman, but it didn't surprise her that Mitch had been there for her grandmother. Strange though, that Gran had never mentioned that he'd been living in the boathouse for the past four years. Rebecca thought back to her yearly visits. Why hadn't she seen Mitch? And why hadn't Gran told her that the 'caretaker' was none other than her former boyfriend? She shrugged, making a mental note to ask him about it. Today's visit to the lawyer had made it clear that her grandmother enjoyed plotting. Even Mitch would agree to that.

She smiled to herself as she thought back to their last school term.

*   *   *

Their friendship, solid from years of mutual trust, had blossomed into a sweet romance during those last few months. His kisses, shy at first, grew ardent, and she had responded eagerly. 'Their spot' was the top of a scarred piece of pre-Cambrian shield at the end of a forest trail. Lying back on the sun-warmed rock, they shared their dreams. Their first kiss had been atop that rock. Even now, the sweetness and innocence of that time left her breathless with the memory. Mingled with their growing awareness of each other was a new, deeper feeling of trust.

Graduation day approached and the hallways hummed with anticipation as students gathered in clusters, talking about the future. Rebecca sailed through those days on a cloud of happiness, fingering the promise ring she wore on a chain around her neck.

If she closed her eyes, she could still see the expression on his face.

They'd been sitting on their spot overlooking the lake, watching the setting sun paint the clouds on the eastern skyline.

"Will you wear this?" he asked, producing a delicate ring. "It's a promise ring."

A small sapphire caught the remaining light and she raised her eyes to his, blinking back tears. "It's beautiful," she said as he slipped it on her finger.

"I planned to give you this on graduation night," he said, laughing nervously, "but I can't wait."

"I'm glad you didn't," she said, holding up her hand. "It's beautiful."

"I thought . . ." He searched her eyes. "I thought that if you have it for a few days, you know, sort of to get used to the idea, that we can talk about our future on graduation night."

Even now, Rebecca had no trouble recalling the excitement she'd felt preparing for the dance, knowing that afterward she and Mitch would plan the rest of their lives together.

The memories were too painful. She tipped the cat from her lap and walked to the screened porch. Mitch was right. There was a lot about him she didn't know. A breeze wafted in from the lake and she shivered, as much from their recent encounter as from the cooling temperature. The attraction that had burned during their school years still simmered. But there were too many unanswered questions, and one heart that still cringed at the painful memories. She peered out into the gathering darkness and shook her head. Why had Gran forced this upon her? Upon both of them? None of it made any sense.

The sound of birds woke her, and she stretched lazily. The morning sun dappled the leaves of the tall tree outside her window. She'd slept surprisingly well, considering the memories she'd allowed herself to relive last night. As her feet hit the floor, she glanced at the dresser, at the small jewelry box she took everywhere. Before she could stop herself, she opened it and rummaged impatiently through the clutter of necklaces and earrings. Ah, there it was, tucked back in the corner where she usually kept it. Taking out the ring, she held it up, turning it in her fingers. She rarely looked at it. It was better that way, she told herself. Because the ring represented the one unanswerable question—what if?

"Stop it," she told herself aloud, and returned the ring to the jewelry box. Padding to the shower, she reviewed what needed to be done today. Bank first, then Mitch. She smiled as she recalled how he had looked at her last night.

But he was her partner, not her lover, and she needed to remember that!

"This wood is very special." Mitch was speaking to a young man as she popped her head into the boathouse later that morning. A worn leather toolbelt hugged the contours of his hips and the muscles of his back and shoulders moved enticingly under a snug T-shirt. "White cedar is not only a beautiful wood, but it's difficult to find, so treat it with the respect it deserves." Faded jeans emphasized his powerful legs, and her mouth went dry at the sight of him.

The teenager nodded and selected a piece of wood. "How's this one?" he asked, eager to please.

"Good choice," said Mitch, moving toward the band saw. He leaned over to switch it on, and spotted Rebecca out of the corner of his eye.

"Rebecca." For one brief moment his smile was for her alone, and then he clapped the young man on the back. "I'd like you to meet Greg Webster. He's going to spend the summer working with me before he makes a decision about apprenticing in boat building."

"Hi Greg." Rebecca threaded her way through the woodworking equipment and offered her hand. "Welcome to our end of the lake." She indicated the bay. "Have you been to Water Lily Bay before?"

"No ma'am." He darted a look at Mitch before shaking her hand. "It's nice and quiet out here."

"Yes, it is, isn't it?" She turned to Mitch. "I came to report on my trip into town."

Mitch glanced at his watch. "Could we do that around noon? Greg and I are due for a break and I could come on up to the lodge."

"Perfect. I think I'll dig out Gran's reservations file and

see how many bookings she's taken for the summer."
With a bright smile, she headed back to the lodge.

Forty-five minutes later they were seated across from
each other in the kitchen. He eyed her warily. "Any surprises at the bank?"

Rebecca scanned the statements. "Gran had eighteen
thousand dollars in her personal account, and a little under
six thousand in the lodge account. Taxes are due on July
15, so if we decide to do this, we can keep things going
over the summer. That's all that really matters, isn't it?"

"If we decide to do this." He stood up and went to the
coffeemaker, taking his time pouring two mugs of coffee.
"Still haven't made up your mind?" He set the mugs on
the table, nudging the sugar bowl toward Rebecca.

Tossing the papers on the table, she stood up, almost
knocking over her chair. Pacing the floor, she gnawed at
her lower lip.

"At the risk of sounding selfish, Gran's request to keep
the lodge open really conflicts with my career. I was
offered the position of head writer a few days before I
left." She ran her fingers through her hair, lifting it off her
neck. "Even though we're on summer hiatus, they expect
a decision soon."

"And if you don't take it?" He watched her carefully.

She shrugged her shoulders. "I haven't thought that far,
but I suppose I could find something else."

"That's a tough one." He cradled his coffee mug
between his palms. "But when it's all said and done, don't
you think you should go for it? Stella was always telling
me how hard you work. This promotion is your reward."

"You sound like my agent." She stopped pacing. "So
you think I should take it, forget about the lodge?" She
held her breath.

"No . . ." He drew the word out. "I didn't say that." He toyed with his coffee cup, not meeting her eyes. "I've seen how Stella's guests feel about this place, and I'd like to go along with her wishes and keep the place open for the summer at least. But we're not talking about the lodge, we're talking about your career. How long before you have to make up your mind?"

"I should let them know soon. A couple of weeks max."

"I wish I could help." His tone had softened. "But this is one decision only you can make." He stood up. "Look, I've got to get back to Greg. What are you doing for dinner?"

She looked at him blankly. "I hadn't even thought about it."

"Okay then. We'll run into town and eat at the diner." He headed out the door and then turned back. "Don't worry—we'll figure it out." He flashed her a smile and then was gone.

She sat staring after him. She seemed to be doing at lot of that these days. Up until a few days ago he had been a faded memory in the scrapbook of her life. Now he was rarely out of her thoughts. It was disconcerting, to say the least. What was even more disconcerting was how much his opinion mattered to her. Because undeniably, it did.

Chapter 3

Changing into her bathing suit, Rebecca grabbed a towel and padded down to the dock. Shading her eyes, she squinted at the sun and moved the chairs so that her back was to the sun, her feet resting on the opposite chair. It was time for some serious thought. The position of head writer for a new television series didn't come along every day, and she'd been about to call her agent and accept the offer when word of her grandmother's death reached her. And now Gran was asking her to give it all up, to stay and run the lodge for the summer.

Her gaze rested on the old building. At any moment, Gran would step out onto the back stairs and wave. She blinked, trying not to let her emotions cloud her judgment. But why not, she asked herself. Maybe it was time she made a decision based on what she knew in her heart to be right. She cocked her head to one side, studying the structure. While basically sound, it could definitely use some upgrading. On her last visit, Gran had mentioned putting on a new roof, and the trim was badly in need of refinishing. She shook her head. It would take more money than Gran had left to bring it back to its former glory. And yet it exuded warmth and character, unlike her brand new penthouse condo overlooking False Creek in Vancouver.

Startled, Rebecca realized that she hadn't thought about her condo since arriving here. Stylishly modern, it was a tangible symbol of her success. Last week, out of the blue, her realtor had called with an offer to purchase—an astounding fifty thousand dollars more than she paid less than a year before. She had declined, her ears ringing with assurances that it would sell 'overnight'.

The whine of a saw broke into Rebecca's thoughts and her gaze slid back to the shoreline and the boathouse, visible through the trees. Male laughter erupted from the boathouse and floated across the water. Mitch appeared to be an excellent role model for Greg. She wasn't surprised. His own father had been abusive and he'd vowed that he'd never follow in that same path. Who better to reach out to the troubled youth in the community?

She probed her memory. When Mitch wasn't learning the craft of boat building, working for the local shipwright, their time had been split between the library and the lake. In bad weather they'd retreated to a corner of the library; Mitch reading the Toronto papers while Rebecca devoured novels. Long before school was out for the summer, their attention shifted to the lake. They spent hours in the canoe, usually with Mitch paddling while Rebecca sat facing him, trailing her fingers in the deep, green water.

Lost in her daydreams, she was startled by the sound of footsteps on the dock. She looked up to see a young woman walking toward her.

"Are you Rebecca?" The voice was surprisingly sweet, considering her unusual appearance. Tight black slacks hugged long, thin legs. A black leather jacket hung open, revealing a short black tank top. Body piercings outnumbered the metal studs on the jacket. The somberness of the outfit was relieved by brilliant fuchsia streaks in the young woman's spiky hairdo. "My name is Ophelia. I worked for Stella."

Rebecca scrambled out of the chair, feeling suddenly as if she'd fallen down a rabbit hole. She managed a smile and held out her hand. "Pleased to meet you, Ophelia."

"Yeah, me too." Her handshake was soft and wary. "Stella told me that you were prettier than the picture she showed me. Now I see what she was talking about." She perched on the arm of one of the chairs. "So, I was wondering about working at the lodge this summer. I mean, are the regular B&B customers coming back, or what?" She nibbled on a fingernail and then guiltily hid the hand behind her back.

Once again, Rebecca found herself being surprised by her grandmother. "Do you mind if I ask you a question?"

"Sure, I guess."

"Did my grandmother ask you to call her Stella?"

Ophelia's smile was shy. "Yeah. It was weird at first, calling an old woman by her first name, but she was way cool." She examined her fingernails. "She used to scold me when I bit my nails. I worked for her the past two summers. I'm going to miss her."

"Me too," Rebecca mused. She was beginning to realize that she didn't know her grandmother very well. She'd chatted gaily about Ophelia without mentioning her appearance.

"She talked about you all the time."

Rebecca didn't think she could bear to hear one more person tell her that. The back of her throat burned, and she fought to keep from crying. "Gran told me about you and what a great help you were but I'm sorry, I can't remember what your duties were. Do you mind refreshing my memory?"

"I cleaned up the rooms and did the laundry. Sometimes I'd help clear away the breakfast dishes if Mrs. Scalia needed help."

"Mrs. Scalia?" The name sounded familiar. Gran must have mentioned her.

"Yes, she used to live in that farmhouse up by the old mill, but she moved away last winter."

"And she was the breakfast cook?" Rebecca hadn't stopped to think about such things.

"Yeah, she was good." Her hand wandered toward her mouth and she pulled it back. "So, what do you think?"

Rebecca raked her fingers through her hair and sat down opposite the young woman. "I don't know, Ophelia. I have to make a decision soon, I know that." She couldn't bring herself to say what she was thinking, which was that she was beginning to feel completely overwhelmed. "It's just that I've never done anything like this before. It's a big commitment."

Disappointment flickered in the dark eyes. "How long will it be until you decide? I mean, should I be looking for another job?"

Rebecca's heart went out to the young woman. "How much did you make in a month working for my . . . for Stella?"

Ophelia shrugged. "I guess it depended on whether or not I worked extra hours. Between eight hundred and twelve hundred dollars a month. Why?"

Rebecca smiled. "I'd like to ask you to wait for a few days. If I don't hire you, I'll pay you five hundred dollars for your inconvenience. How does that sound?"

The young woman backed up. "Oh no, I couldn't do that. I couldn't take money for not working."

"But it's only fair. I'll know by the middle of next week, latest."

"Well okay, I guess. But you don't have to pay me if you decide not to open. That wouldn't be fair." She twisted the silver rings on her left hand. "Not fair at all."

For the first time in days, Rebecca felt some of her old confidence returning. "I think it's perfectly fair. I'm sure Gran has your number somewhere, but would you mind giving it to me?"

Ophelia handed her a piece of paper. "I had it written out, just in case."

"I like that. You know how to think ahead." Rebecca smiled and took the paper. "I'll call you one way or the other, and thanks for coming out."

Stella had converted the small sunroom off the kitchen into an office. Rebecca settled in and was surprised to find the files efficiently organized. The reservations were logged in a ledger, with the first arrival two weeks away. A quick scan of the bookings showed that dozens of return guests had already been confirmed. She opened a pile of mail and found two more requests in the stack. A quick perusal of paid invoices from last year offered a clear picture of which vendors Stella had preferred. The file folders were well worn, making the new one stand out. It had no name written on the tab, and she pulled it out, her interest piqued.

The top sheet was on the letterhead of the municipality. Rebecca noted the date—April first. Gran would have appreciated the irony. The form was a building inspection report, accompanied by a letter. Rebecca scanned it. The report strongly recommended a new roof and an upgrade to the electrical service. The letter was official notice that the building inspector would make a second inspection in September, after the tourist season, at which time he would make further recommendations. Rebecca wondered if someone in an equivalent position in a large city would be quite so considerate. Despite being couched in friendly terms, the message was clear. Upgrades would soon be mandatory. She looked further. Underneath the correspondence from the municipality were quotes from a roofer and from an electrical contractor. She sucked in a surprised breath. The figures were enormous. She needed to talk this over with Mitch.

Leaning back, she watched a grey squirrel leap nimbly from branch to branch outside the window. The only squirrels she saw in Vancouver were in Stanley Park. Her gaze fell on the reservation ledger spread out on the desk. The lodge was a special place to the people whose names were so carefully entered in that book, just as it was to her. But could she put her career on hold to honor her grandmother's wishes? It was a lot to ask.

The roar of the Harley announced Mitch's arrival. Startled, Rebecca looked up from the desk. She had spent the last two hours looking in every file in the small office and the time had slipped away.

"Hi there," she said from the top of the stairs. "Are we going on that?"

"Why not?" He smiled up at her. "Although you might want to rethink that outfit."

Rebecca looked down at the short skirt she had put on after swimming. "I'll be right out."

Slipping into a pair of jeans her spirits lifted and she felt carefree for the first time in months. Sparkling eyes looked back at her as she checked her makeup in the mirror. The soft rumble of the motorcycle outside was a siren song. She picked up her purse and then tossed it back on the bed. Tonight she was completely free.

"Hop on," he said, his eyes approving her outfit. "And hang on to me."

"I've never done this before," she said nervously as she settled behind him. She didn't know where to put her hands.

"You'll do fine." He took her hands and placed them firmly on his abdomen.

He felt so good! He smelled of soap, and his hair was still wet from the shower. It took all the control she possessed not to lay her cheek against his broad back.

"Ready?"

"Oh yeah," she replied breathlessly. "I'm ready."

"Move with me," he said over his shoulder, and she squeezed her eyes tight, glad he couldn't see the expression on her face.

The wind whipped her hair back from her face as they leaned into the turns, and far too soon they pulled up in front of the diner.

Rebecca eased off the bike and stood with her hands on her hips. "That was fun," she said. "I didn't realize what I've been missing."

"Yeah," he said with a rakish grin. "There's a lot of that going on around here."

His hand slid around her waist. "Come on, let's get something to eat."

"Hiya Mitch." The waitress greeted him effusively, and Rebecca felt a quick jab of jealousy. It was ridiculous, she knew, but she couldn't help it. The woman was old enough to be his mother, for goodness sake.

"Midge, I'd like you to meet Rebecca Lambert. Becky's grandmother owned the lodge at Water Lily Bay."

Keen brown eyes took in Rebecca's flushed cheeks and windblown hair. "Good to meet you, Rebecca. Mitch is one of our favorite customers." She lowered her voice. "Young Billy is in the kitchen tonight. We might make a cook out of him yet." She turned to Rebecca. "When Mitch first asked us to take on one of his young men from the youth outreach program we weren't sure, but it's worked out very well. Of course he thinks Mitch walks on water, but other than that, he seems to have his head screwed on right." Her face softened. "You're doing good work, my lad. All right now, enough of that, do you want to hear the specials?"

Rebecca popped the last piece of garlic bread into her mouth and looked down at her empty plate. The grilled chicken and Caesar salad had been worthy of any fine restaurant. "That was delicious," she said, reaching for her tea.

Mitch had tucked into a plate of meat loaf, mashed potatoes, and vegetables. He smiled at her across the table. "It's great to see a woman with a good appetite. Sharon used to drive me crazy with her picky eating." He shot her an apologetic look. "Sorry. I didn't mean to bring her up."

Rebecca cradled her cup between her hands. "You're still friends, I hope. You know, for Scott's sake."

He gave a rueful smile. "It's tough sometimes, but we try to behave ourselves when Scott's around." He shook his head as though trying to rid himself of a bad memory. "I've been negotiating for more time with Scott through my lawyer. I've always had him for Christmas, but I'm trying to add a month each summer, plus spring break." He stared into his coffee cup. "He's growing up so fast, I'm beginning to feel that I don't know him very well.

He's coming to a summer camp at Lake Simcoe in about a week and when that's over he's going to stay with me for our two weeks together. I was wondering if I should take him somewhere."

"What's your gut instinct? What do you think he'd like to do?"

He sat back as Midge cleared their plates. "I don't know. But I think he'd be more relaxed at the lake."

"Then that's what you should do." She nodded her head firmly.

He sat back in the booth and studied her openly. "You're right, of course." A smile crept across his face. "Sensible as well as beautiful. A good combination."

She blushed. Another thing she'd been doing a lot of lately. She busied herself with the teapot.

"Can we talk about Gran's will for a minute?"

He opened his hands. "Sure."

"There's the thing with the ashes." She felt for her purse. "Oh darn, I didn't bring my purse. Anyway, I was wondering if you'd like to go to Bermuda this weekend." Her heart pounded. "We don't have to stay long, but it would be nice to get that out of the way."

Something molten surfaced in his eyes and then slid away. "Would you like to arrange it? Just let me know where and when."

Anticipation surged through her body. "Okay," she said. "That settles that."

She placed an imaginary check beside an imaginary list. "Next item. How do you feel about Gran's request that we not sell the lodge for a year?" Her eyes searched his. "Can you live with that?"

"Becky." His voice was low and fierce. "I live there. I love living there. It's everything I ever wanted. So the answer is yes, I can live with that."

She was taken aback by the intensity of his answer and stared at him as if seeing him for the first time. Slowly, she lowered her head and made another check.

"I saved the hardest one for last. Keeping the lodge open. Do you still feel the same way?"

"Absolutely. I've had four wonderful years out there. It's the least I can do for Stella. I'll gladly keep the boats in order and take care of the maintenance and all the outdoor stuff. Shucks ma'am, I can even wash dishes or check in the guests if you need help."

"Be careful what you promise. I'm only beginning to grasp everything that's involved. It's a lot of work. I went through all the files this afternoon and I have a handle on the business aspect of the B&B, but actually doing it is another thing."

"Listen." His voice softened. "I know it's a difficult decision, and whatever you decide, I'll understand. All I can say is that I know we can do it. Whatever you decide, I'm with you all the way."

"Even if I decide to go back?"

"Even then." His eyes held hers. "All the way."

Flustered, she changed the subject. "There's something else. Did you know there was a building inspection this spring?"

His eyes narrowed, and he sank back into the corner of the booth. "Come to think of it, I saw the building inspector's truck, but I didn't hear any more about it."

"That's what I thought." Rebecca bit her bottom lip. "You can read the report, but basically he notified her that the lodge needs a new roof and a new electrical service."

Mitch grunted. "That doesn't surprise me. There's not enough power for me to run more than one piece of equipment at a time. And as for the roof . . ." He shrugged. "It's needed replacing for a few years."

Rebecca nodded. "At the risk of sounding like a procrastinator, we don't really have to make any decisions now, do we?"

"No, we don't." He slid out of the booth, and a slow smile transformed his face. "Besides, I'm too busy looking forward to a weekend in Bermuda."

Mitch looked out the window. The island lay below them, a lush green gem in the shimmering ocean.

"Oh look! There it is." Rebecca turned to Mitch, eyes bright with enthusiasm.

She had been quiet on the flight, and he hadn't disturbed her. He was surprised and somewhat relieved to find that he could still tune in to her moods, if not her thoughts. It was clear that she still had not come to a decision about Stella's requests. To tell the truth, he was feeling a little off-kilter himself. Despite the amount of time he'd spent with Stella, he hadn't had the slightest idea what she was up to. It still made no sense to him. What did make sense was the depth of his attachment to the lake, to the lodge, and especially to the boathouse. He'd paid his dues in the world of business, and he was glad to be free of it. There was always a market for well-crafted handmade boats. He was now in the enviable position of accepting only those projects that appealed to him, and being his own boss left him time to work with the youth outreach program. Life was good. The only thing that could make it better would be if Scott could live with him. He shook his head slowly. Perhaps in a few years.

"Mitch?" Rebecca was looking at him curiously. "You seem a million miles away."

"Huh?" His eyes slid past her. The aircraft was on final approach. "Sorry. What were you saying?" He nodded to the flight attendant as she collected their glasses.

"I was pointing out what I think was our hotel, but we're past it now." She pressed her forehead to the Plexiglas. "We're not even on the ground yet, and I'm already wishing that we were staying longer. It's a pity to come all this way for just two nights."

Her words tumbled over each other, reminding Mitch of the effervescent schoolgirl he'd known so many years ago. He looked out over her shoulder, smiling at the memories.

The wheels touched down, and she turned to him slowly. "Why are you smiling like that?"

His heart felt as though a large hand was squeezing it. "I was remembering," he said. "Let's leave it at that."

"I hope you don't mind, but I booked us at one of the smaller hotels." Rebecca took charge as they passed through baggage claim. "And someone from the hotel will meet us and drive us to the hotel."

Mitch nodded, content to let her take over. They were on their way to the hotel within minutes.

"I'm sorry but we can't offer you adjoining rooms on such short notice." The desk clerk was apologetic. "But I think you'll be pleased. They both overlook the beach."

"I'm sure they'll be fine." Rebecca glanced at Mitch. "Shall we meet at the bar in about half an hour? We can plan what we're going to do."

Mitch followed the porter up a wide set of stairs, and Rebecca followed another porter along a cool hall to her room. As he swung open the French doors she gasped in delight. Beyond her lanai, soft pink sand glowed in the afternoon light, and the turquoise ocean sparkled invitingly.

She unpacked rapidly and slipped into a cool sundress. Studying her reflection in the bathroom mirror, she decided that she could use a day at the beach. Ever since hearing about her grandmother's death, she'd been on the go. She ran her fingers though her hair, grateful that the weather wasn't too humid. With a light step, she made her way to the bar overlooking the beach. The atmosphere was relaxed and festive. One couple sat away from the rest of the crowd, engrossed in each other and seemingly in love.

Her throat closed up as she recalled her last relationship. She and Rob had been going out for about six months, and they enjoyed each other's company, finding that they shared many interests. But when he'd suggested an exclusive commitment, it was the beginning of the end. Panicked at the thought of a serious relationship, she had ended the friendship, and had bought her new condo just weeks later. Since then, she hadn't dated, in spite of the efforts of her co-workers to 'fix her up'.

"May I get you something to drink?"

Rebecca was startled back to the present by the smiling face above her. "Sparkling water please, with a twist." Looking up, she saw Mitch standing at the entrance to the bar. "Make that two, please," she said, her voice suddenly husky.

He was dressed in tan trousers and a pale blue shirt, open at the throat. As usual the sleeves were rolled up, and he looked deliciously male. Spotting her, his eyes lit up and he threaded his way through the tables. Several sets of female eyes followed him appraisingly and Rebecca experienced a jolt of proprietary jealousy.

"So here we are." He slipped easily into the chair across from her and sat back, studying her.

"I ordered for us," she said as the waiter appeared with their drinks.

"You look great, Becks." He continued to study her, and she fought to control the blush that threatened to creep up her neck. "Happy and relaxed." He picked up his drink and saluted her. "Welcome back."

He closed his eyes as he drank, and Rebecca watched his Adam's apple bob up and down. The motion was purely masculine, and her gaze slid lower to the dark chest hairs poking out through the neck of his shirt. She shivered involuntarily, and swallowed along with him, her throat suddenly dry. An image of Rob flashed through her mind and she wondered how she could ever have been attracted to him. By comparison, Mitch was vibrantly alive and all male. She inhaled sharply as she recalled the perfection of his body as he hauled himself out of the lake that first evening.

"A penny for your thoughts."

His voice broke into her daydream and this time she did blush. "Some thoughts are better left unspoken" she said with a smile. She had to stop these childish fantasies about him.

"Should we rent a scooter to see the island?" She leaned forward eagerly. "I understand there are some wonderful beaches."

"Sounds good." He sobered. "But why don't we get a cab right now and ask them to take us to a deserted beach where we can scatter the ashes. That will leave us all day tomorrow to explore. What do you think?"

"Sounds like a plan."

Mitch held up his glass and waited until she clinked hers against it. "Here's to Stella," he said softly. "She was a grand old girl."

"Yes, she was, wasn't she?" Rebecca's eyes misted over. "I'll miss her."

The driver knew the perfect spot and promised to wait. It was windy on the beach and the sand whipped against their legs.

"Let's go down there to that little headland. We can give them a good send-off."

Rebecca didn't think she could have managed it without Mitch. "Do you want to say anything?" he asked quietly when they reached the slight rise.

"Just good-bye." Tears pooled in her eyes but they were tears of joy. Gran and her darling Hugh were finally together. The wind snatched the ashes and scattered them along the pink sand where they mingled and disappeared forever.

Mitch steadied her with an arm around her waist and led her back to the waiting taxi. "Okay?" he asked tenderly.

"Yeah." She smiled up at him. "Surprisingly, I am."

Chapter 4

A gentle evening breeze stirred the air in the dining room. Soft pools of candlelight illuminated the diners, and Rebecca raised her eyes to find Mitch watching her. "Sorry I'm not very good company tonight. It's just that scattering the ashes was so final. I'm just beginning to realize that she's really gone."

"Yes, but you did what she asked." He sipped his coffee. "And corny as it sounds, I like to think that she's at peace now."

Rebecca blinked back tears and stood up abruptly. "If you don't mind, I'd like to be alone tonight." She gestured at the remains of their meal on the table. "Thanks for keeping me company."

He followed her out into the lobby. "Becky." He reached out and captured her hand. "I'll see you in the morning."

She nodded and walked slowly to her room, unaware of the lingering gaze following her progress.

* * *

Mona Ingram

Entering her room, she crossed to the French doors and threw them open. Rolling her head back and forth, she rotated her shoulders, easing the tension that had been building all day. Waves hissed up onto the beach and then retreated, leaving a fine sheen of water dappled with moonlight. With a burst of energy, she changed into shorts and a blouse. Quickly locking the doors behind her, she crossed the coarse grass and sank her toes into the sand. A gurgle of pleasure escaped from her throat and she walked slowly, heading for a pile of rocks at the far end of the beach.

Mitch set down his glass and smiled at the woman beside him. She had slipped onto the adjacent barstool moments after he came in.

"Do you have to go?" She ran her tongue slowly across her bottom lip. The invitation was clear.

"I'm afraid so." He was surprisingly unmoved. Signing the bar tab, he said goodnight and ran up the stairs to his room. It was only 10:30, and he wasn't the slightest bit tired. Resting his forearms on the balcony railing, he looked out toward the ocean. A cloud covered part of the moon, but the water still shone with reflected light. It was too beautiful to waste. He kicked off his shoes and dug out an old pair of shorts and a faded T-shirt. A run along the beach should tire him out. Maybe he'd be able to sleep after all.

He walked past the swimming pool and ran down onto the beach, testing the shoreline for the strip of sand packed hard by the surf. Looking both ways, he decided the beach was empty, and set off at a slow jog. The air was cool, and he barely broke a sweat. At the end of the bay he turned and retraced his steps. The entire beach was only about half a mile long, but that didn't matter. He decided to run as far as the rocks at the far end and then do it once more.

His thoughts returned to Becky. In spite of his marriage and several liaisons over the years, no woman had reached into his heart and his mind the way that Becky had. Tonight when her eyes misted over he'd wanted to wrap her in his arms and reassure her. He wanted to wipe away the tears that threatened to roll down her cheeks and kiss that stubborn mouth until she relaxed and melted against him. With a quick shake of his head he pushed those thoughts aside, pulling up about a hundred feet away from the rocks at the end of the beach.

Rebecca sat hunched on the rocks, arms linked loosely around her knees. The sorrow that enveloped her earlier had passed and she relaxed, letting her thoughts drift from one happy memory to another—and of course those memories included Mitch. She couldn't help but wonder what her life would be like today if things had turned out differently on their graduation night. She had been so proud of her graduation dress. It had been her first dress with a low neckline, and Gran had lovingly placed her own string of pearls around Rebecca's neck. She fingered her neck now, as though expecting to feel the pearls.

A movement down the beach caught her attention. Someone was jogging along the high watermark with long fluid strides, moving like a well-trained athlete. He stopped suddenly, turning to face the water and she let out a sigh of relief, realizing it was Mitch.

"Mitch? What are you doing here?"

He squinted in her direction, and at that moment the

cloud moved away from the moon. "Oh, there you are." He glanced around. "Becky, you shouldn't be out here by yourself."

"I'm not by myself." Her eyes held a hint of mischief. "You're here."

He shook his head. "You know what I mean." He took a few steps closer. "Do you mind if I join you up there?"

She patted the rock beside her. "It's not as good as our spot at home, but you're welcome to share it."

He settled onto the rock beside her and his thigh brushed against hers. "I was just thinking about you," he said, scanning the water in front of them.

"Me too," she said, glancing at him out of the corner of her eye. "I was thinking about all the memories we shared when we were young." She laughed nervously "Those were such innocent times. I mean in comparison with what the kids get up to nowadays."

He didn't answer her right away; she sat quietly, studying him. His face had matured, and a surge of resentment swept over her as she was reminded that she had missed the years that turned him from a teenager into the intensely appealing man who sat beside her. She wanted to cry out that it wasn't fair; she wanted to pound her fist against his solid chest and berate him for leaving her. She wanted him to know that she'd been forever changed—unable to give her heart as a result of what he'd done.

He reached down and picked up a small piece of rock, examining it in the pale light. His beautiful fingers rolled it over, and Rebecca realized that he wasn't really looking at it, but that he was somewhere far away.

"I want to tell you about that night." Mitch stared straight ahead. "But I have to back up a bit. Dad was being abusive to my mom. I used to see bruises on her all the time. I told you how he behaved to me, but I didn't tell you about my mom because I was too ashamed to admit that I couldn't protect her." He was silent for a moment, remembering. "One day it got so bad I threatened to kill him if he ever touched her again."

He looked at the rock in his hand as though wondering how it got there. Rebecca sat wordlessly beside him, willing him to continue.

"He drank a lot." A short, mirthless laugh escaped his lips. "That's an understatement—in the last few years I was at home I rarely saw him without a drink in his hand." With a quick flick of his wrist he tossed the rock into the foamy surf.

"Anyway, on our graduation night . . ." he turned to her, his expression haunted. "On our graduation night he must have started drinking early in the afternoon, 'cause by the time I got home to pick up my money for the corsage, he was completely wasted. He started threatening Mom, and I tried to stop him."

Rebecca found she was holding her breath, waiting for him to go on.

"I got in a couple of good punches before he recovered from his surprise. It's probably just as well I wasn't all that strong because believe me, I wanted to do him some serious damage . . . I was that mad." He shot a quick glance at Becky. "He backhanded me across the room, and when I came to he was gone. He took all the money I'd saved—including the money for your corsage—and went to the bar. I wanted to follow him and have it out, but Mom pleaded with me." His eyes followed the slow curl of foam on an approaching wave. "She knew how much that night meant to me, but even so, she begged me to leave town right away. She was afraid for me, afraid that something bad would happen if I stayed any longer. I didn't want to listen. I knew you were waiting, and the idea of leaving was tearing me up." He closed his eyes, and Rebecca felt a tear slide down her cheek. "I still don't know how she talked me into it, but she drove me to the bus depot and stayed beside me every minute. I remember trying to convince her to leave him. Shortly after we got there, the bus left for Toronto and I was on it and we were pulling out before it even sank in that I hadn't called you." He sat very still, lost in thought. "Somehow, even though I was just a kid, I knew that things would go easier for Mom if I wasn't around. He died a few months later, as you probably heard." Rebecca nodded. "He got drunk and passed out on the railway tracks. You think stuff like that only happens in the movies."

So that's what happened! Rebecca's body suddenly felt light and she gripped the rocks to keep from floating away. She didn't know whether to laugh with relief, or to cry at the cruel twist of fate that had kept them apart. Nothing could erase the pain and bewilderment she had experienced that night, but knowing the circumstances eased the dull ache in her heart that had never quite gone away.

The memories flooded back, and her voice cracked. "I sat there in my graduation dress all night, waiting for you. I was sure you'd come." Another tear rolled down her cheek and he reached forward to brush it away, but she pulled back. If he touched her now, she'd come completely undone. And anyway, she needed more answers.

"You broke my heart," she said, her voice cracking. "Why didn't you ever get in touch with me?"

Mitch was taken aback and his face showed it.

"Why do you look so surprised?" She brushed away the tears, angry with herself for losing control. "You of all people must have known how I was feeling. Every morning I'd wake up and tell Gran that I'd be hearing from you, that you'd explain." The empathy she'd been feeling just a few moments before was quickly being replaced by a burning anger that had been simmering for years. She jumped up and brushed off her shorts. "I'm going back to the hotel."

Mitch stared after her for a moment, then scrambled to his feet. He needed a few seconds to compose himself. All of a sudden everything was so clear. Stella hadn't given her his messages after all. All those phone calls! And she'd never given Rebecca his letters! That's why he hadn't heard from her. He nodded to himself as he followed her along the beach. It was all beginning to make sense.

Should he tell her the truth? Should he tell her that he hadn't been able to stay away, that he'd come back to town only two weeks after leaving? He paused, his mind reeling. He had to tell her in such a way that she wouldn't resent her grandmother's interference. Stella had been the only loving adult figure in Rebecca's life. He couldn't shatter her illusions now.

He caught up to her and grabbed her arm.

She shook free and continued walking, glaring back at him over her shoulder. "What?" she said harshly. "What?"

"I came back for you," he said softly.

She stopped so abruptly, he almost ran into her. "You did?" Her face was momentarily radiant, then her eyes narrowed, peering at him suspiciously. "Why didn't Gran tell me?"

He shrugged, and spread his hands in supplication. "I don't know, Becks. You'd gone out west to school by then. This is only a guess, but she probably wanted to encourage you to make new friends." He recalled how Stella had refused to give him Becky's address. "She always had your best interests at heart."

A slow smile transformed her face. "So you came back to see me. What were you going to say?"

He grinned down at her. "I wish I could remember the speech. I practiced it for the longest time, I remember that."

She stood looking up at him, not budging when a wave hissed up the beach, nibbling at their feet.

"I do remember that I stopped at the flower shop and paid for the corsage I wasn't able to pick up on graduation night. And while I was there I bought you a single rose." His eyes softened at the memory. "I think I must have read somewhere that it would help with an apology. Anyway, I took a deep breath and went out to the lodge."

He reached out and brushed his fingers against her cheek. This time she didn't pull back. "I wanted to tell you how sorry I was and ask your forgiveness. I was sure that if I came in person, you would eventually forgive me. I was prepared to do some serious groveling, if necessary." And the direct approach had seemed like the only way he'd get past Stella, he recalled.

"Is it too late?" He looked boyishly hopeful.

"Too late for what?" Her voice was little more than a whisper.

"Too late to ask you to forgive me." His eyes roamed over her face, coming to rest on her lips.

"I don't know." Her heart thundered inside her chest. "But I'd like to hear it. What would you have said?"

"Well." His palm cupped her cheek. "I would have told you how beautiful you are, and how it tore me up to leave town that night." He swallowed. "I would have asked you to wait for me until I could get on my feet."

"Is that all?" Her eyes shone in the moonlight.

"No." His voice was husky. "I would have kissed you."

She tilted up her face. "Show me, Mitch."

He lowered his head, his lips brushing her mouth with a tantalizing touch. Softly at first, as though she might pull away, then his mouth slanted over hers with an aching intensity. She moaned softly, slipping her arms around his neck until she could feel every inch of his body. Eleven years vanished in an instant.

They broke apart at the same time and stood gasping in the surf, looking at each other with a new awareness.

"That would have been some apology," she said, her breath coming in short little gasps.

"And that was some acceptance." His voice was thick with emotion. "Perhaps I should misbehave, so I can apologize again."

"Not if it takes eleven more years." She chuckled softly, then turned away, taking a few steps back toward the hotel. "Although it was worth waiting for."

"What did you say?" His long legs brought him level with her in a few strides.

"Nothing." His revelations were turning her world upside down, shaking out thoughts that were far too personal. Thoughts that had never stopped taunting her. She tossed her head and kept on walking, determined not to let him break through the defenses she'd so carefully erected. Defenses she wasn't ready to let down. At least not yet.

"So what happened to your Mom?"

"She remarried. He's a great guy and he treats her well. They live in Thunder Bay."

"I'm glad for her, Mitch." She continued walking. "After everything she went through, she deserves some happiness."

"Listen, about tomorrow. I inquired at the front desk, and they'll make us a picnic lunch."

"That sounds wonderful." Her bungalow loomed behind a cluster of trees. "There's my room. I'll say goodnight."

She was sure he was going to reach for her, and was disappointed when he shoved his hands in his pockets. This was a good time to ask him about something that had been troubling her.

"Mitch, why haven't I seen you around when I've been visiting? You've been living in the boathouse for four years, and I had no idea."

"But you always came at Christmas."

"Every year since I left. It became a tradition between Gran and I."

"And I have every Christmas with Scott. We go somewhere warm and just hang out together. Last year we went to Epcot Center. It's become a tradition for us, too." He shifted his feet in the sand. "Now I have one for you. Why didn't you ever visit in the summer?"

Tears stung the back of her eyes. "I'm not sure," she whispered, her voice barely audible. "I told myself it was because Gran was busy with the B&B, but I think it was the memories." She avoided his eyes.

He stood looking at her, his face in the shadows. "Goodnight, Becks." His voice was as gentle as a caress. "We can't change the past, but it's up to us what happens from now on."

"You're right," she said with a faint smile. "See you in the morning."

"Everything looks different today." Rebecca held her face up to the sun as Mitch loaded the picnic hamper onto the scooter. Towels and a beach blanket cushioned the hamper.

He glanced at her appreciatively. She wore a loose, gauzy blouse over her bikini top, and a pareu from the gift shop was wrapped around her waist. "You can say that again," he murmured. With her hair tied back and a smile on her face, she looked years younger.

"It's not a Harley," he said, revving the motor. "But it'll do." He tossed his head. "Hop on sister, we're going for a ride."

They browsed leisurely through the market, admiring the local crafts amid the usual souvenir offerings. Mitch bought a T-shirt for Scott and a pair of surfer shorts. "He'll be the coolest dude at camp this summer," he announced proudly as they walked back to the scooter.

Rebecca adjusted the floppy hat she'd purchased, pulling the string around her chin. "Do you think I'll get to meet him?"

Pleasure bloomed in Mitch's eyes. "I'd like that. He's a good kid."

They toured the island slowly, and with one voice they expressed their delight at finding a small, deserted beach.

"This looks good." Mitch paused.

"Oh Mitch, this place is perfect."

They laughed easily together. The sky was an intense blue, softened by wisps of cloud high overhead. After spreading their blanket in the shade of a tree at the edge of the beach, they romped like children in the gentle surf. Mitch went out beyond the breaking waves and swam a couple of laps parallel to the beach while Rebecca dried off, following every stroke of his long, tanned arms as they flashed through the sparkling water.

His kiss last night had shaken her, awakening the feelings that had lain dormant for so long. When she'd opened her eyes this morning, it was the first thing that entered her mind. Although the sun was warm, she shivered imperceptibly. She was treading on dangerous ground.

Mitch came running up the beach, water streaming from his body. She assessed him openly, admiring the strong swimmer's shoulders and the tightly ridged muscles of his abdomen. She swallowed as he loomed over her and tossed him a towel.

"That was refreshing," he panted, dropping down beside her. "Now I'm starved."

Rebecca wiped her mouth with the back of her hand. "I can't believe they forgot the napkins." The chicken had been crisp and tender, and it had tasted heavenly as they ate it with their fingers. They washed their hands in the ocean and Rebecca lay back on the blanket, relaxed and content. The sun filtered through the leaves, dappling them with small coins of light. Her thoughts returned to his revelations of last night and she sat up abruptly, turning to face him on the blanket.

"I'd like to hear the rest of your story," she said, eyes telegraphing her curiosity. "Thanks to Gran you know everything that's happened to me since . . ." she waved her hand as though brushing away a cobweb. "Since that night. What happened after you got on the bus? Where did you go in Toronto?"

She settled herself cross-legged on the blanket, watching him expectantly. A leaf fluttered down from the tree, landing on his legs.

"Mom had sent me off to live with her brother." A smile of remembrance lit his face. "Uncle Dave was a real character. He and Mel were good to me. They even loaned me the bus fare when I came back looking for you."

"Mel?"

"Yeah. Aunt Melanie. Anyway, Uncle Dave helped me to find my first job." He picked up a handful of sand and watched it sift through his fingers. "I bounced around a bit at first, and then I settled down and worked two jobs. I worked on a construction crew during the day and at night I worked for a building-maintenance firm." He grinned. "That's a euphemism for janitor. Anyway, the company I worked for had a contract with some of the big Bay Street trading firms." He seemed to sit up straighter. "Do you remember all those afternoons we spent in the library at home? You read novels while I read the Toronto papers?" She nodded. "Even back then I was interested in the stock market and how it worked. As I was emptying wastebaskets, I noticed that these firms had job postings in their lunchrooms. I saw a posting for an entry-level position, and I applied for it. It meant quitting my day job, but it was worth it." He picked up another handful of sand. "I took every course they offered and kept advancing through the ranks. In a little over three years I was an assistant to their top-producing broker."

"And did you enjoy it?" She leaned forward eagerly.

"Yes and no." He squeezed his hand and the sand spilled out in a fine stream. "It's a pretty cold business. I saw fortunes come and go so quickly." He opened his fingers, staring at the grains of sand sparkling on the palm of his hand. "I stuck with it as long as I could, and then four years ago I quit to move back home."

"And you went to visit Stella."

"Yeah. Speaking of Stella . . ." He draped his arms over his knees, and his eyes turned thoughtful. "When you mentioned finding out about your family history, I remembered something. She used to write in what she called her journal. From the way she talked, I got the impression that it was something she'd been doing for quite a few years."

"I don't suppose you know where she kept it?" Rebecca couldn't recall ever seeing her grandmother with a journal. "I looked all through the desk in the kitchen when I was reviewing the B&B business, and it wasn't there."

He shook his head. "No, but it's a pretty big place. You'll run across it eventually, I'm sure."

She nodded her agreement. "We're getting off the subject. What happened next? When did you learn to build boats?"

He leaned forward, his eyes suddenly bright. "It's the best thing I ever did. You remember how I used to enjoy working part-time at the boatworks when I was a kid? Well, one weekend, Dave took me out to Centre Island and I met Rollie Cubbon, a shipwright. Rollie was an amazing craftsman. I think he'd forgotten more about building boats than most shipwrights will ever know. When I saw the work he was doing, I knew I had to learn more. I worked with him every chance I got, and I was privileged that he was willing to pass on his knowledge." He held up his hands. "Don't get me wrong. I'll never be half as good as Rollie, but I learned enough skills to build a decent runabout."

"Did you build the one sitting beside the dock at home?" She recalled the classic lines of the boat and the rich mahogany woodwork.

"Yes, that's mine."

"Wow." She looked at him with new respect. "You're good."

"It's easy to be good when you're doing something you love. Ever since I set up the shop, there hasn't been a day that I don't feel like working. There aren't many men, or women for that matter, who can say the same." He lay back on one elbow and studied her. "How about you? Do you like your work?"

She brushed a few grains of sand from the blanket, gathering her thoughts. "I like the craft of it. I enjoy doing the research, and I especially enjoy writing dialogue." She grinned at him sheepishly. "Although I suppose that's obvious, since I'm a screenwriter."

"I sense there's a 'but' coming."

She looked up. "You're right. What I dislike is the endless rewrites. Sometimes I feel like someone else is pulling the strings." She stared unseeing at the blanket, her fingers absently tracing the pattern. "There are times when I see my life as a series of scenes. It's as if I'm standing back behind the camera watching it unfold." She raised her eyes. "I'm not in it. I'm more of an observer than a participant."

Mitch watched her steadily, and she drew strength from his silence. "It frightens me." A tentative smile played around her lips. "Maybe that's why I've been waffling about taking on the new position, even though it's a wonderful opportunity. I want to take control of my life, as well as my work." She peered across at him, surprised by the understanding in his eyes. "Does that make sense?"

"It makes perfect sense." He turned back toward the ocean. "What else would you try? Would you still write?"

"I hope you don't think I'm foolish, but I'd like to try my hand at a novel. I've had a few ideas percolating around in my head for some time now."

"It would be a shame not to reach for your dreams." He stood up abruptly as a stiffening breeze showered leaves down on them. "It looks like our day of leisure is coming to an end." He pulled on his shirt and shook the sand out of the blanket.

Rebecca picked up her sandals, wiggling her toes in the sand. It was warm and soft, and she hated to leave. "This has been a perfect day," she said dreamily. "And it's good to know we're friends again, as well as partners." She tossed her beach towel over her shoulder and picked up the hamper, heading toward the scooter.

Chapter 5

"Let's order champagne." The aircraft had reached cruising altitude, and the cabin attendants were serving drinks. "I think we should celebrate."

"Fine by me." Mitch eyed her curiously. "May I ask what we're celebrating?" He raised his glass.

She turned in her seat. "We're celebrating the opening of Water Lily Bay for one more summer. I called the producer this morning and explained the situation to him. We're on hiatus for three months, and he said I should take the time off. They'll e-mail me if anything comes up in the meantime."

"Are you sure?" His eyes searched her face. "What about the position of head writer? Has he withdrawn the offer?"

"Surprisingly, no. I asked for two weeks to decide on that and they agreed." She studied the bubbles rising in her glass and missed the flash of pain that darkened his eyes for a moment. She sighed. "I think I always knew I'd stay for the summer. One look at those names in the reservation log book and that was it."

"In that case, welcome back."

"The only thing I'm really concerned about is a breakfast cook." She glanced over at him. "Do you have any ideas?"

"What happened to Mrs. Scalia?"

"Ophelia says she moved away. For a while I considered doing it myself, but I don't think that would be wise. I have a feeling I'll be busy enough without trying to cook as well."

"I think you've got that right. Why don't we go to the diner tonight and ask Midge? She may have some ideas."

"Sounds good," she agreed quickly. "Can we go on the bike again?"

He turned to her, feigning shock. "Why Miss Becky, you've turned into a biker chick."

"And what if I have?" She looked at him saucily.

He picked up her hand and brought it to his mouth. "I like it," he murmured against her fingers, the warmth of his lips heating every nerve ending. "I like it a lot."

"Gee Honey, let me think about that for a few minutes." Midge stood beside their table as Rebecca looked at her expectantly. "Meanwhile, I'll place your order."

She headed toward the kitchen, and Rebecca looked at Mitch. "I hope she can think of someone. Our first guests will be arriving on the weekend."

Mitch watched her align the cutlery on the table. Her cheeks were flushed from the bike ride, and her face was framed in a mass of curls. His fingers tensed around his water glass, and without realizing it, he shook his head, warning himself against becoming emotionally involved.

"You're shaking your head." She looked alarmed. "Do you think she won't be able to think of anyone?"

"No, that's not it at all." He glanced toward the kitchen.

"Midge knows everyone around here. She'll come up with a couple of names."

As predicted, three names were delivered along with their food. "Mind you, I'm not sure if they're available," she warned. "But give them a call and find out."

"You're wonderful." Rebecca's relief was evident as she studied the list. "I'll call them first thing in the morning."

Mitch smiled to himself as he swept up the sawdust. Passing on his knowledge to Greg was surprisingly rewarding. He was confident that Rollie would have approved.

Had it been only a couple of days ago that he'd been in Bermuda, telling Becky about learning his craft? He changed into his bathing suit. The lake beckoned, and he walked barefoot to the end of the dock, tossing his towel on one of the chairs. Diving cleanly into the clear water, he surfaced fifteen feet away and eased into a rhythmic crawl. The water was cool and refreshing, and he swam for twenty minutes, then hauled himself up, stretching out on one of the chairs in the warmth of the late afternoon sun.

Had he done the right thing by not telling Rebecca about Stella's interference? Strangely enough, he didn't feel any lingering bitterness. That was surprising, considering how he hated to be manipulated. After recovering from the shock of learning that Rebecca had never received his letters, he'd managed to put it out of his mind . . . until now.

It had been a typical spring day when Mitch came back to town four years ago. The roads gleamed from a recent rain, and flower bulbs pushed hopefully through the cold earth. He drove through town on his Harley, gathering curious glances from the few people who noticed him.

Before he realized it, he found himself at Water Lily Bay Lodge.

"Lordy! Is that you, Mitch?"

Stella had been sitting on the front porch, gazing out over the lake. She insisted that he join her for a cup of tea, and after his initial surprise at the warmth of her greeting, they settled in for a long chat. He found her to be bright and articulate, with a delightful sense of humor.

"Will you stay for dinner?" she asked, trying unsuccessfully to hide her loneliness.

Mitch accepted, and over dinner he told her about his love of boat building. After apple cobbler and a cup of tea, Stella had grabbed a flashlight, insisting that he follow her along the path to the boathouse, as if it were the first time he'd seen it. He didn't have the heart to remind her that he and Becky had been the ones to take in the boat and the canoe every winter, and launch them again in the spring.

He hadn't needed much encouragement to turn the boathouse into a workshop. Stella was adamant that if he did the work to transform the loft into a studio, he was to live in it rent-free, in exchange for a few chores during tourist season. She encouraged him in his work with the youth outreach program, and he developed a genuine respect for her independence. Listening eagerly to her glowing reports about Rebecca, he'd often wondered why Stella had accepted him after all this time. And now, knowing that she'd withheld his letters, he was even more confused. He shook his head. It wouldn't be the first puzzle about Stella to remain unsolved.

"Hi partner." Rebecca stepped onto the dock, carrying two dark brown bottles. "Remember how we used to love this orange drink? They're making it in bottles again and I thought of you."

"I'm flattered." He reached for the glass and his fingers brushed against hers, sending his heart into overdrive. This had to stop!

"So how are you and Ophelia getting along?" He'd noticed her earlier in the day.

"Surprisingly well. It's amazing how much we got done today. Two rooms are ready to go, and we work on the rest of the house in between times." Her eyes sparkled with enthusiasm. "I hired a breakfast cook. Her name is Lisette and she worked at a B&B in the Laurentians. I think we'll get along just fine."

"That sounds good. When does she start?"

"That's the part that makes me a bit nervous." Rebecca bit her bottom lip. "She has to go back to Quebec for a few days to take care of some business and she plans to come back the day before our first guest arrives." She brightened. "But I checked her references, and if she's even half as good as what her last employer said, we're lucky to find her."

"That's good." His eyes slid down her bare legs, lingering on the pale pink polish on her toenails. "I'll be ready too. The boats are in the water and right now Greg and I are busy refinishing the picnic tables. Then we'll put a fresh coat of paint on all the chairs and we've added one more chore to the list. We're going to re-paint the trim on the lodge." His voice gentled. "It's going to be great, Becks. I'm proud of you."

"You know what we need?" Ophelia ran her hand along the top of the sideboard. "We need one of those long skinny things for the top of this." She turned to Rebecca. "You know what I mean."

Rebecca smiled. "Yes, I do. It's called a runner. I thought we had some, but I haven't seen them around."

Ophelia tugged at the ring in her eyebrow. "I think they're in that chest in the attic. I'd look for you, but Greg is giving me a ride home." She indicated Greg's battered van, which stood idling in the driveway.

Rebecca glanced at her watch. "Oh my goodness. You should have told me it was this late." She made shooing motions with her hands. "Run along and have fun. I'll look for it later." The two youngsters were going to a concert in Bracebridge.

Watching them drive off, Rebecca felt a surge of affection for the teenager. She turned back into the great room and paused, proud of what she and Ophelia had accomplished together. The beautiful old wood flooring gleamed, and inviting groups of chairs awaited the first guests. Rebecca had splurged on several large plants, and ferns hung from the ceiling while ivies competed for space with Stella's African violet collection. The room exuded the warmth and caring that had made the lodge a perennial favorite.

With an unsettling sense of déjà vu, Rebecca stood at the bottom of the long narrow staircase leading to the attic. She flicked on the overhead light, which did little to dispel the darkness of the stairwell. Memories assailed her as she climbed the stairs.

The golden afternoon sun filtered through the west window, highlighting the objects that stood in its path. Rebecca pulled a rag from her pocket and rubbed the window, muttering to herself. It needed a good cleaning, as did the rolltop desk next to it.

The old familiar objects were just as she remembered. An old wicker baby carriage, minus a wheel, stood precariously in a corner, tennis rackets in wooden frames sticking out at odd angles. Chests, boxes, a dress dummy, old lamps, snowshoes, and hundreds of books were stacked under the eaves, leaving a clear space in the middle of the room for browsing. Remembering her reason for coming up here, Rebecca tugged on the doors of the old wardrobe, which had been retrofitted with shelves. The scent of lily of the valley floated out to meet her, swamping her with memories of Gran. It had been her grandmother's favorite. The runner was neatly ironed and folded, as though waiting to be called to action once more.

Rebecca hesitated. She wasn't ready to go back downstairs yet. A faint sound at the foot of the stairs beckoned her, and she looked down to see her cat with one paw on the staircase.

"Pekoe, you lazy boy. Come on up and explore with me." Her eyes lit on a box of old games, and her heart swelled at the memory of her grandmother playing patiently with her on cold winter nights. The cat peered cautiously around the corner and ran across the floor, rubbing contentedly against her leg. She picked him up and buried her face in the soft fur. "So many memories," she whispered, her eyes misting over. "They're all here."

Her eyes fell on a battered trunk. Gran had always been lenient when it came to trying on the clothes inside. It had been Rebecca's treasure chest, her rainy-day escape when she was little. Setting the cat down, she fell to her knees in front of the trunk and lifted the lid, wondering if it still contained the ability to transform her into a princess.

The items in the trunk had been repacked with care. The shallow tray on top held gloves, evening bags, scarves, and several pert little hats. The accessories were wrapped in tissue paper, and she greeted each item with a cry of recognition, as she would an old, familiar friend.

Lifting out the tray, she placed it carefully on top of a nearby chest. Inside the trunk was where the real treasure lay. Stella had saved her 'party' clothes, and they were exquisite. These too had been wrapped in tissue, and Rebecca reached inside, unfolding the delicate white paper from the item on top.

She pulled back abruptly. "I don't believe it," she whispered, looking into the trunk. "She saved it."

The single long-stemmed rose had been carefully dried. A couple of leaves lay in pieces beside the stem, but other than that it looked as though it had been placed there yesterday. The scent was as delicate as the flower, and her heart ached for the young man who had brought it to her. Placing it carefully on top of the old rolltop desk, she went back to the trunk, slowly turning back the next layer of tissue. The years fell away as she looked down at the exquisite dress, folded and waiting for her. She dropped down onto her knees and reached into the trunk, running the tips of her fingers over the delicate fabric.

"I'd forgotten how beautiful it is," she said aloud, gazing at the intricate workmanship on her graduation dress. Wiping her hands on her shorts, she picked it up and walked to the large mirror in the corner, holding the dress in front of her. The pale ivory fabric was studded with delicate pink roses, intertwined with green leaves and stems. The heart-shaped neckline was flattering, and she swayed back and forth, making the softly layered skirts swing with the movement. Holding the dress aside, she looked at herself critically. She could still fit into it—she was certain. There was one way to find out. Shivering with anticipation, she laid the dress carefully on top of the trunk and slipped out of her clothes.

The dress slid over her head and settled onto her body, the fabric whispering against her skin. Goosebumps appeared along her arms, and suddenly she was afraid to look in the mirror. Reaching back, she zipped it up as far as she could, the built-in foundation cupping her breasts, urging them ever so slightly above the low neckline. Walking on bare feet, she crossed the attic, daring herself to look into the mirror.

What she saw startled her. The afternoon sunlight, diffused by the layer of grime on the window, created a misty, golden aura that wrapped around her, transporting her back to the night of her graduation. Bowing to the reflection in the mirror, she picked up the hem of the skirt and took a few steps back into the room, eyes locked on her image.

"Becky. Are you up there?" Mitch's voice rose from the bottom of the stairs.

Rebecca looked about wildly as his footsteps came closer. There was nowhere to hide. Resolutely, she tossed back her hair and stood her ground as he bounded up the last steps.

"I was wondering if you wanted . . ." He came to an abrupt halt, eyes flaring as his gaze moved slowly from her bare feet to the top of her head. He reached out and steadied himself against the doorjamb, seemingly speechless.

The expression on his face slowly changed from one of shock to one of pleasure. A broad smile lit up his face, and Rebecca felt a flush creep up her neck as the smile moved to his eyes, which now lingered on the neckline.

"What were you saying?" She pirouetted in front of him, thoroughly enjoying herself.

"I can't remember." His voice was husky. "My God, Becky, you look beautiful." His eyes returned to her feet. "Like a barefoot princess."

"Yes, well . . ." It was almost, but not quite, worth the

wait to see the expression on his face. "I can't find the shoes Gran bought me to go with the dress." She motioned to the trunk. "They may be in here."

"It doesn't matter. You look delicious." Her pushed away from the doorway and circled her, devouring her with his eyes. The smile turned to a frown. "Wait a minute. Is this your graduation dress?"

She turned to him, surprised to see him struggling with his emotions. "Yes, it is." She spoke softly, tenderly. "But it's okay, Mitch. It doesn't hurt so much anymore." Placing her hand against his cheek, she looked into his tortured eyes. "You suffered just as much as I did. No . . . more. Much more."

He shook his head, as though emerging from a trance. "I guess so. But there's one thing I have to do." He grasped her by the shoulders, turning her around to face the mirror. "You need help with your zipper."

His breath warmed her neck in soft little puffs as he stood behind her. His fingers found the tab of her zipper and eased it up. He looked over her shoulder at her reflection, hands resting on her shoulders. "I wish we had some music." His voice seemed to come from a distance. "I'd like to have at least one dance with you in this dress." Becky's breath caught in her throat as she met his eyes in the mirror.

"Why don't you check that old record player in the corner?" She scarcely recognized her own voice. Her heart was pounding against her ribs, and she wondered if he could feel it. "I think it still works."

Mitch lifted the old 33rpm record and blew off the dust. Her eyes fastened on his lips, and a jolt of bittersweet longing raced through her body. "You're gonna love this one," he said, turning on the machine and lowering the arm. "It's perfect." He walked back to her and bowed formally. "May I have this dance?" The rich, mellow tones of *Smoke Gets In Your Eyes* filled the attic.

Rebecca moved toward him slowly, as though in a dream. He smiled down at her and then gathered her in his arms. She laid her head against his chest with a contented sigh, feeling his heart thudding in her ear. They swayed to the music, giving themselves up to dreams of what might have been.

"What are you thinking about right now?" His voice held a hint of sadness.

She tilted back her head, her breath catching in her throat. "I was thinking that this is almost as good as a graduation dance. Funny, isn't it, how life hands you all those precious moments when you're too young to appreciate them." She allowed her gaze to roam openly over his face. "Don't let this go to your head, but you're far more interesting now than you were when we were kids."

He twirled her slowly, then pulled her back into the circle of his arms. "And you're more beautiful." His fingers brushed the side of her neck, and then slid up into her hair. She closed her eyes, moving slowly to the music and wishing the record would never end.

When she opened her eyes he was looking at her, his intentions clear. She lifted her lips and his hand cupped her head, pulling her closer. He kissed her with a tenderness that made her heart ache for all the lost years. Eleven years of wondering what might have been were distilled in their embrace, igniting a depth of emotion she didn't think possible. Somewhere in the back of her mind warning bells went off and they pulled apart, gasping for breath.

Mitch sucked in a ragged breath of air. "We can't do this, Becks." He pulled back and gazed into her eyes. "Although I dreamed of it often enough. Even when I was convinced you didn't want anything to do with me." His face took on a faraway look. "It was thinking about you that kept me going. And then, when the memories started to fade, you became an unattainable fantasy."

His words swept over her like a healing balm. She spoke haltingly. "I thought . . . back then, and for many years afterward . . ." She placed her palm against the side of his face. "I thought I'd misunderstood your intentions."

He shook his head sadly. "You didn't misunderstand. But those days are gone, and we can't pick up where we left off. Here, let me show you something." He turned her around to face the mirror. "See those two people? They're adults now." She squirmed to turn and face him, to look at him directly, but he held her firmly in his grasp and leaned over her shoulder, meeting her eyes in the mirror. "For the time being, we're working together, but we both know our lives are going in different directions. The past was . . . well, the past. This is now." He groaned. "I wish I could say it better, but you understand, don't you?"

She blinked rapidly, fighting back tears. "Mitch Burton, I hate it when you make sense." She stepped out of his embrace, afraid that she would shatter if he touched her again. Perhaps she wasn't completely healed after all. "You're right, of course," she murmured, looking everywhere but in his eyes.

Her words hung in the air between them. There was nothing left to say. He turned and left the room.

Rebecca listened as he went down the stairs and through the kitchen to the back door. The screen door slapped and moments later the roar of his motorcycle broke the silence of the summer evening. Unaware that the sun had slipped below the horizon, she stood in the darkening attic, her fingers curled tightly in the folds of the dress. Tears streamed silently down her face as the sound of the motorcycle faded into the distance.

Mitch forced himself to relax his grip on the handlebars as he slowed at the only stoplight in town. He hadn't known that he possessed the strength to do what he'd just done. It had been self-preservation, pure and simple. Finally, after years of self-doubt, he had his life just the way he liked it. To get involved with her now would be inviting more heartache when she went back to Vancouver. It was much better this way . . . wasn't it?

"Good morning!" Ophelia breezed into the dining room where Rebecca was folding napkins. "The concert was great."

"That's nice." Rebecca kept her head down.

Ophelia's hand strayed to her mouth then she pulled it away. Her nails were actually growing. "Is everything okay?" She stepped closer, placing her hand on Becky's arm.

Rebecca turned, forcing what she hoped was a bright smile. "Everything's fine."

Ophelia didn't push any farther. She looked around. "So did you get the runner yesterday afternoon, or shall I run up and get it now?"

Rebecca looked up, startled. "I don't know what's the matter with me, I forgot to bring it down." She shoved the pile of napkins toward the teenager. "Finish these for me, would you? I got . . ." Her hands fluttered in front of her face. "I got looking at old stuff and forgot to bring it down."

Rebecca stepped into the attic, and it was as if yesterday's emotions still hung in the air. She'd been in a rush

to get out of the attic last evening and had left her graduation dress tossed over the open trunk lid. Folding it carefully, she wrapped it gently in the crumpled tissue, and
closed the trunk. She'd been foolish to even consider
starting up with Mitch again. Staring down at the lid of
the trunk, she acknowledged that she would do well to
keep a lid on her emotions as well. Better yet, they should
be locked up, where they would be protected from any
further bruising.

Now I'm being melodramatic, she thought, as her eyes
wandered over the collection of old items in the room.
She wandered over to the desk, absently caressing the
worn wood. It was better this way. She couldn't afford the
heartbreak of becoming too involved, especially when her
other life was waiting for her in Vancouver. With a quick
shake of her head, she broke off her reverie.

She was about to turn away when the dried rose caught
her attention. She'd forgotten all about it. It had slid to the
back of the desktop and was lodged against the wall.
Reaching back to pick it up, her fingers brushed against
something. She felt again. An old key was hanging on a
small nail at the back of the desk. She fitted it into the
desk and rolled up the oak slats, revealing a variety of
compartments and several small drawers inside. Here
again, the lingering scent of lily of the valley greeted her,
and she squinted her eyes, as though trying to see into the
past. Vague images floated through her memory, and as
they came into focus, she recalled finding her grandmother up here on several occasions.

She was hesitant to look at the papers tucked so carefully into the slots. This was her grandmother's private
desk. An old brass inkwell gleamed softly in the center
section, and Rebecca ran her fingers over the smooth surface, feeling oddly comforted.

Three drawers made up each pedestal, and she succumbed to her curiosity, slipping the key into the top lock. It turned smoothly, and she pulled out the drawer, peering inside. A black leather-bound book sat on top, and she picked it up, opening it to the first page. *'My Journal'* it read, and her curiosity overcame her. She started reading.

"Hey, boss." Ophelia's voice broke into her reading sometime later. "There is someone on the phone. Can I take a reservation for this weekend?"

Rebecca looked guiltily at her watch. Forty-five minutes had passed like nothing.

"Sure," she called down the stairs. "As long as it's not for more than two rooms." She sat back down in the old wicker chair, her thoughts churning. It looked like the lodge would be full for the first weekend of the season—Gran would have been pleased. She glanced down at the journal in her hand. There was some fascinating stuff in here. Another journal was in the same drawer, and she took it out, then locked the desk, returning the key to its hiding place. Remembering to pick up the runner, she went back downstairs.

Chapter 6

"**I** think we'll be finished by tomorrow," said Ophelia, as they checked over the last guest bedroom later that afternoon. "That gives us a free day to get ourselves ready."

"I'm beginning to get worried about our cook." It felt good to voice her concern. "I was hoping to hear from her by now."

Ophelia refolded the fluffy towels. "I'm sure she'll get back from her holiday in time."

"You're right." Rebecca smiled at the youngster's confidence. "I'm just nervous, that's all."

"No way." Ophelia drew back. "You're the coolest. Everybody knows that."

Rebecca laughed. "Oh yeah? And who is everybody?"

The teenager blushed. "Well, Greg thinks you're hot. And Mitch told him that you've always been the brightest girl on the block." She dropped her eyes. "Those were Mitch's words, not his."

Rebecca shook her head. "I'm not so sure about that, but thanks for the vote of confidence." She slipped her arm around Ophelia's thin shoulders as they walked into the kitchen. "I don't know how I would have managed without you. You've been a big help."

"Do you want me to stay?" The black-lined eyes were concerned. "I mean, I could stick around if you like. You know, keep you company."

Rebecca looked fondly at her helper, thankful that Gran had been able to spot the potential in the youngster. "Thanks Ophelia, but what I need right now is to be by myself. I'm going to climb up to what used to be my favorite spot when I was a kid. It's a perfect spot for thinking." Her eyes drifted to the desk in the corner, where the journals waited. "And maybe I'll do some reading as well."

"Okay then." Ophelia pushed open the screen door. "I'll see you tomorrow."

Not wanting to waste a moment, Rebecca gathered up the journals and closed up the lodge. Surprisingly, the path was still passable. She climbed for several minutes, emerging on the crest of the hill, on a piece of rock smoothed by an ancient glacier. A breeze lifted her hair, swirling it around her face and she laughed out loud, raising her arms to the sky with joyous abandon.

"Now I'm really home," she said, drinking in the familiar view. The lake sparkled below her and the roof of the lodge was barely visible through the trees. The sun was still a couple of hours above the horizon and she settled into a depression in the rock, smiling to herself as she realized that it wasn't as big as she remembered. She was soon immersed in the journals, oblivious to the beauty of her surroundings.

Mitch scratched Pekoe behind the ear and the cat raised its head, looking at him sleepily. The animal had wandered into the workshop earlier in the day, settling down in a sunny spot by the front window. "I'd better go and see your mistress," he said, running his hand along the soft fur. The cat blinked twice then returned to the serious business of sleeping. Mitch wandered along the path to the lodge, wondering what he would say.

Over the years, his memories of Becky had faded. As a teenager he had believed himself in love with her, but as the years passed, those memories had blurred, changing from reality to fantasy. Then she'd walked back into his life—a beautiful, desirable version of her former self— and he'd been unprepared for the strength of his response. He should have seen it coming, but common sense had deserted him. Like a fool, he'd allowed himself to hope that she was home to stay. In spite of everything he'd said, he wanted her more than ever. But that was as far as it would go. If she should decide to stay—and he hoped with all his heart she would—it would have to be her idea. He would not ask her to give up her career; this time it was Becky who would have to come back. He could wait.

Knocking for a second time, he leaned over the porch and peered in the kitchen window. The lodge appeared deserted. Her car was behind the building, in its usual place. He tried the door, frowning when he discovered it locked. What was it that he'd overheard when Ophelia came to meet Greg after work? Something about Becky being out of sorts today and going off to think. That was it! She'd gone up to their spot. With a faint smile on his lips, he started hiking, wondering if she'd notice that he'd kept the trail open. Nowadays he only made the climb a couple of times a year, but keeping the trail open was his way of showing the faith.

Rebecca stared out over the tops of the trees, lost in thought. The realization that she'd never truly known her grandmother came as quite a shock. The second journal was in her lap and she looked down at it with a bemused smile, running her fingers absently over the leather binding.

Stella had started the journals after Hugh died. As a record of her thoughts and her life, they were remarkable. Rebecca gnawed on her lower lip. During their time together her grandmother had shared many thoughts with her, but never the ones in these journals.

She was surprised to learn that as a young woman, Stella had wanted desperately to study medicine. Her disappointment was eloquently chronicled in the journals, and Rebecca's frustration mounted as she read her grandmother's words. Even after being married for many years, Stella still chafed at having been held back from the education she so fervently wanted.

Covering the years from Hugh's death until the time that Rebecca went away, the journals captured the heartbreak Stella endured when her daughter and son-in-law were drowned on the Great Lakes, and her initial hesitation about raising her granddaughter. Rebecca's heart softened as she learned of her grandmother's uncertainty, her worry that she may be 'too old-fashioned'. In later years, her concerns became more focused. With increasing frequency, she wrote of her determination that Rebecca should have whatever education she desired. Stella constantly worried that her granddaughter would get married before 'spreading her wings'. With a profound sense of sorrow both for grandmother and herself, Rebecca finally understood why she had been sent across the country to school.

Hugging the journal to her chest, Rebecca watched the clouds change from incandescent pink to bruised purple. The beauty of the sunset, like happiness, was fragile and precious. Nothing ever stayed the same. She had learned that only too well.

* * *

She heard the whistling, and her heart suddenly felt lighter. In spite of her tangled emotional state, she smiled. It was their signal; advance notice to whoever was there first that the other was approaching.

He pushed aside the branches and stopped abruptly on the smooth rock. For a moment they stared at each other.

"I had a feeling I'd find you here." His voice was deep and intimate, and Rebecca was glad he couldn't see the quickening of her pulse.

He took his usual position beside her, arms draped over his knees. Breathing easily after the steep climb, he stared out over the lake.

Rebecca glanced at him out of the corner of her eye. His face was deeply tanned, and a fine stubble on his cheeks made her want to reach out and touch him, to confess how much she cared. But she couldn't.

"I've been thinking about you all day," he said quietly. He picked listlessly at a piece of lichen. "We shared everything up here." He turned to her and a brief smile lit his eyes. "Do you remember?"

Her heart bounded around inside her chest. "Yes, of course." Memories surfaced, and she gestured to the island in the middle of the lake. "I remember how you promised me you'd buy Osprey Island one day." She lowered her head. "I remember everything we shared. Sometimes the memories are so vivid I feel like I'm a child again."

"I know what you mean." An unmistakable longing textured his words. "But we're not kids any longer."

"No, although sometimes . . ." She let her words trail off.

"Do you ever wonder what would have happened if we'd gone to our graduation dance?" The question was voiced so softly it caught her off guard. She glanced up to find him staring at her intently. "Do you think we'd still be together?"

Rebecca raised her hands, then dropped them to her side. "I don't know, Mitch. I really don't know. All those 'what ifs'" She smiled softly. "Although I couldn't begin to count the number of times I wondered the same thing myself." She picked up the journals. "Some things are becoming a bit clearer, though."

"What's that?" He glanced at the journals.

"I found Gran's journals today. I've been sitting up here reading them."

She related the highlights of what she'd read, including the resentment and regret that Stella had so eloquently detailed. Her hand rested on the journals as she came to the final entry, as though maintaining contact with her grandmother. "When I read these it's almost like she's here again. I can hear her voice and once or twice I even imagined I could smell the lily of the valley perfume she used to wear." She smiled faintly then continued. "I wish I'd known how she felt about my education. It might have made things easier. Knowing the truth makes all the difference in the world." She hugged the journals, as though they would protect her.

His gaze drifted out over the lake and came to rest on Osprey Island. "You've got that right," he said softly. Standing up, he offered her his hand. "Come on, we'd better get going. It's getting dark."

"Can I ask you something?" Ophelia stood uncertainly in the kitchen doorway. They had agreed that the lodge was as ready as it could be for the guests that would arrive the day after tomorrow.

"Of course." Rebecca forced herself to stop worrying about the nonappearance of the cook. "What is it?"

"Well . . ." Ophelia examined her fingernails. "Do you think a person should tell another person if they . . . you know, really like them?"

Rebecca smiled. "This sounds serious. Let's get some iced tea and sit at one of the picnic tables outside."

The teenager sat hunched over, dunking an ice cube into her drink with her finger. "I guess you know I've been going out with Greg." She looked up, and Rebecca nodded. "I think he really likes me, but he never says anything." She fidgeted in her seat. "We went to that concert the other night and he just took me home and dropped me off." Her voice dropped to a murmur. "He didn't even kiss me."

"How long have you been going out? You just met him this summer, didn't you?"

"Yeah, but . . ." She examined her fingernails, suddenly agitated. "You don't mind talking about this stuff, do you? I can't really talk to my mom."

"No, I don't mind at all. I've had those same feelings myself, but it seems like a long time ago." Rebecca's eyes softened. "I was friends with someone for ages before he even kissed me. When it finally happened, it was really special, because by then I knew him."

"Was he nice?" Ophelia lifted her glass, staring intently at Rebecca over the rim.

"Oh yeah." The magic of those days was so real it seemed to hang in the air like a heady perfume. "He was very special."

"Were you in love with him? Did you tell him?" The teenager leaned forward eagerly.

"I'm not sure I knew what love was back then, but yes, I fancied myself in love with him." She stilled, surprised that the old pain could still make her catch her breath. "Then he left town suddenly, and I didn't see him for years. In spite of the way he hurt me, I've been looking for a love like that ever since. We were always so honest with each other. And that trust is still there, even after all this time."

A silence settled over the table, broken only by the wind in the tops of the trees.

"But we were supposed to be talking about you, not me." She looked into the teenager's eyes. "You're bright, and you're attractive. Any young man would be honored to have you as his girlfriend. But you don't have to rush into anything. Get to know him a bit better before you declare yourself. If he cares about you, he'll still be around at the end of summer."

"Why doesn't he say anything?" Her face crumpled. "Maybe he doesn't really like me after all."

"Ophelia." Rebecca reached out and laid her hand over the teenager's. "Men are just different, that's all. They don't express their feelings like we do. Give him time." She glanced toward the boathouse. "By the way, where is he?" A small frown creased her brow. "It's been very quiet over there today."

"Mitch had to go away for the day, so Greg has the day off."

"Really?" Rebecca tried unsuccessfully to cover her surprise. "He didn't mention it."

"It was Mitch, wasn't it?"

Ophelia's voice was softly tentative, and Rebecca wondered for a moment if she'd heard correctly.

"It was Mitch you fell in love with, wasn't it?"

Rebecca started to protest, then nodded silently. Her gaze wandered back to the boathouse. "Yes," she said simply. "It was Mitch."

"Wow." Ophelia's eyes widened, and a new respect dawned in them. "He's so hot."

"Ophelia!"

"But he is! Have you noticed his body?"

A vision of Mitch in his swimsuit filled her mind. "Yes, I've noticed." She rolled her eyes, trying to lighten the mood. "He was swimming in the lake the first night I arrived. Believe me, I noticed."

"Wait a minute. You said you've been looking for a love like that all your life. What are you waiting for?"

"I wish it were that simple." Rebecca squared her shoulders, trying to put her constant doubts into words. "That was the fantasy. This is reality. Right now, my goal is to open this place for summer and honor the reservations Gran accepted. So for the next little while, the lodge comes first."

"Huh." Ophelia drained her glass. "Do you think you guys will ever get back together? You know, like you were before?"

"I don't think so. We've been apart for a long time and we've both had other experiences." Rebecca wondered why she was explaining herself to the girl, but it felt good to verbalize her thoughts. "We're partners. That's all."

"But you'd like to, wouldn't you?" Ophelia immediately lowered her eyes. "I'm sorry," she murmured. "That's none of my business." She busied herself picking up the glasses. "I'll drop these off in the kitchen on my way home. See you on Saturday morning, bright and early."

She ran lightly up the stairs, and Rebecca followed her progress, lost in thought. *Did she want to 'get back together' with Mitch? Yes. And no.* She took a deep breath of pine-scented air. It was going to be a long summer.

The screen door slammed, and Ophelia waved as she pedaled away on her bike. Torn between conflicting emo-

tions, Rebecca welcomed the one constant in her life—
the operation of the lodge.

Running her fingers over the surface of the freshly
painted picnic table, she acknowledged that Mitch had
kept his part of the bargain. Groups of Adirondack chairs
hugged the lakeshore and clustered in the clearings under
the pines. The lodge was ready, inside and out. Crimson
red geraniums in clay pots marched down the front steps,
brilliant splashes of color in the shade of the tall pines.

But there was something missing. The lodge seemed
lifeless without Mitch nearby. In a normal day, hours
could pass when she didn't see him or hear the whine of
a saw from the direction of the boathouse. Then she
would look out and catch a glimpse of him and her heart
would beat a little faster. With him gone she felt incomplete.
Summer hadn't even started yet and she was
already missing him. What would happen when she went
back to Vancouver, to the pressures of her career? She
wasn't sure she wanted to find out.

The first guests arrived mid-morning, and Rebecca
didn't get a chance to look at her watch until late afternoon.
One room remained vacant but by tomorrow every
room would be occupied by returning guests. Rebecca
thought wryly that they probably knew more about the
routine of the B&B than she did. In a rare break, she
watched Don and Elsie Meldrum sauntering hand in hand
along the lakefront. The couple had informed her on
check-in that they had recently celebrated their fifty-third
wedding anniversary.

The telephone rang, startling her out of her daydream.
"Water Lily Bay Lodge" she answered, watching the
older couple settle into the chairs at the end of the dock.

"Rebecca?" Lisette's French accent sounded more pronounced than usual. "It's Lisette. I've had a . . . what you call . . . a breakdown. The mechanic told me he'd have my car fixed by tonight, but now he says no." Her distress was palpable. "I am so sorry, Rebecca, but I won't be there to cook breakfast tomorrow."

Rebecca felt a fine sheen of perspiration break out on her forehead. Today had been so busy that she hadn't had a chance to worry about not hearing from her new cook. She took a deep breath. "When will you be back?"

"I'll be back around two o'clock in the afternoon. Even if I have to leave my car here and come on the bus, I'll get there. But what about tomorrow morning?"

Rebecca laughed and it sounded shrill, even to her own ears. "I guess I'll just have to do my best." Her thoughts raced. "But listen, Lisette, are you going to be all right tonight? Is there somewhere you can stay?"

"Yes, there is a motel just off the highway. I am so sorry. I am really looking forward to working at the lodge."

"Don't worry." Rebecca sounded a lot calmer than she felt. "If it's the worst thing that happens, we'll have had a good summer."

Lisette laughed, her relief obvious. "Thank you for not being angry. I'll see you tomorrow."

"Right." Rebecca hung up the phone and sat down heavily on one of the kitchen chairs. Looking around, she tried to control the panic churning in her stomach. She rarely cooked breakfast for herself, let alone for a houseful of guests!

"Hi, boss!" Ophelia yanked open the screen door. "I just thought I'd stop by and see how everything went today." She fingered a black cord around her neck. "I sure didn't expect to find you sitting down."

Rebecca focused on her assistant. "You're not going to

believe this, but Lisette just called. Something happened to her car on the drive back and she's not going to make it."

The teenager sat down on the opposite side of the table. "Ohmygosh." Her eyes darted around the kitchen. "Do you know how to cook? I mean, I watched Mrs. Scalia, but all I ever eat at home is cereal or toast." She lowered her voice and leaned forward. "What are we going to do?"

Rebecca was touched that the youngster had included herself in the problem. She smiled weakly. "We'll manage. Somehow." Her heartbeat started to return to normal. "Wait a minute. I wonder what Gran would have done?"

"You mean after she laughed and said something about life's little surprises?" Ophelia filled two water glasses from the cooler and set them on the table. "She would have said what you just said." She held up her glass in a toast. "We'll manage. Now, how many people are we talking about?"

"Ten. Five of the rooms are occupied." Rebecca looked around the kitchen as though a solution would present itself.

"Come on, it'll be fun. Besides, these people are like old friends. They like us already."

Once again, Rebecca was thankful for Ophelia's presence. "You're pretty sharp for a teenager, you know." She noticed an unusual sparkle in the dark eyes. "Hey, what's up with you?"

Ophelia blushed, and her hand went to the cord around her neck. "Greg gave me his ring last night." She held it out for Rebecca's inspection. "Cool, huh?"

"Very." She watched as Ophelia tucked the ring back underneath her tank top. "What does it mean?"

"It means that we don't go out with anybody else." She pretended to examine her fingernails. "Now all we need is for Mitch to give you a ring."

An image of Mitch slipping the delicate sapphire ring

on her finger flashed before her eyes, and then she dragged herself back to the present. "Oh no, you don't!" she laughed, wagging a finger at her lively assistant. "Let's get through tomorrow's breakfast first."

"I'll be here at six thirty." Ophelia and Rebecca had spent an hour checking supplies and planning breakfast. "I'll set out everything but the hot food, and when you have it ready, I can carry it out. It's going to be fine."

"I'm beginning to think so, too." Rebecca walked her to the door. It was a good excuse to look for signs of Mitch. His absence irritated her. As half owner of the lodge, surely he could at least be present on their opening day?

Always aware, Ophelia noticed her agitation. "It must be something important. He's really proud of what you're doing, you know."

"What do you mean?" Rebecca forgot her anger for a moment.

"Well, a couple of times when I've been waiting for Greg, he's talked about how not very many people would do what you're doing. You know, taking time off from your job and running the lodge." Stopping halfway down the steps, she looked back. "Now I know why Stella was so proud of you." Embarrassed, she ran down to her bike and pedaled away.

"Will you be spending the night in Toronto?" Mitch's lawyer slid the papers back into the file on his desk.

Mitch glanced at his watch. He'd promised to take Scott to a Blue Jays game, but he should still be able to get home by midnight. He smiled to himself. Home. That was how he thought of the boathouse. Rebecca's face floated before his eyes and he forced his attention back to the conversation.

"No, I have to get back tonight." He glanced at the file. "So, do you think she'll agree? I've been asking for this additional time for several years and I'd almost given up hope."

The lawyer cleared his throat. "I don't think I've ever seen a father with more determination to spend time with his son. It's been six years now and you've never wavered. I admire your tenacity. May I offer you a word of encouragement?"

"I could use some." Mitch leaned forward.

"I've been doing this for many years, as you know. You'd be happily surprised at how often these young lads choose to live with their fathers when they reach their teens and they're free to choose. I've seen it happen over and over again. Especially when they know their father wants to spend time with them." He stood up, extending his hand. "I'll let you know as soon as it's official, but it looks like you'll get that extra time."

Mitch's throat was tight as he shook hands. "Thanks again, Mr. Carmichael. I appreciate everything you've done."

He replayed the conversation with the lawyer on the way home. There were so many things he wanted to do with Scott! As things stood right now, they just barely got comfortable with each other before it was time to take him back. He couldn't wait to share the news with Rebecca.

He should have told her he was leaving, but he'd expected to be back by dinnertime. When he'd asked Sharon if he could take Scott to a ball game, he hadn't dreamed she would agree. He smiled ruefully. Those scalped tickets had cost a fortune, but it had been worth it for the few extra hours with his son and to watch his excitement at the ball game.

He cut his motor and glided silently to his spot beside the boathouse. The parking area behind the lodge was crowded and would likely remain that way through most of summer. Now that the guests had started to arrive, the days would pass quickly. He hung his helmet on the bike and stood staring thoughtfully at the lodge.

What would happen at the end of the summer? Was it too much to hope that Rebecca would stay? Stella wasn't here any longer to keep them apart. As a matter of fact, she'd done her best to throw them together. His eyes were drawn to the small attic window. The memory of Rebecca in her graduation dress shimmered through him like a mirage. He steadied himself against a tree, fingers clutching at the rough bark. "Get a grip, Burton." He spoke aloud, his voice hoarse. "You're acting like a lovesick teenager."

A breeze whispered through the rushes along the lakeshore and he turned his face toward the water, breathing deeply. This is where he belonged. He could only hope that Rebecca felt the same. He knew one thing for sure. No matter how eager he was that she return for good, he wouldn't push her. She had to want to stay—it was that simple. He walked slowly into the boathouse, knowing that no matter how long it took, he would wait for her.

Chapter 7

"They're all nice people," Rebecca spoke aloud as she showered quickly the next morning. "So why am I so nervous?"

She'd spent the remainder of the evening peering out of the kitchen window, watching for Mitch's return. In spite of her increasing concern at his absence, sleep had come almost instantly when she finally crawled into bed around eleven.

Between the pines, early morning sunlight danced on the surface of the lake. Ophelia's bike was propped against a tree in the yard, but she was nowhere to be seen. "At least she showed up," Rebecca muttered, trying unsuccessfully to stop thinking about Mitch.

Ophelia chose that moment to come bouncing into the kitchen. "Hi, boss," she said brightly. "How did you sleep?"

"Surprisingly well." Rebecca wrapped an apron around her waist, fingers fumbling nervously as she tied it. "Where were you? I saw your bike outside."

She waved airily. "I was around front, watering the

geraniums. And," she added casually, "checking to make sure that Mitch is back."

Rebecca looked up. "And is he?"

"Of course." She smiled a smug little smile. "He wouldn't desert you on your first morning." Stepping back, she eyed Rebecca's outfit. "By the way, you look nice this morning. I like that long skirt." She collected an armful of cereal boxes and headed for the dining room, brimming with youthful confidence.

Switching on the coffee urn that they had prepared last night, Rebecca hummed to herself. With Mitch here, her confidence had returned. She chose two cantaloupes for slicing. She could do this!

She barely felt the knife slice into her finger and then things started to move in slow motion. Blood welled up and flowed from the cut, dripping off the end of her finger and splattering on the floor. She stared at it in disbelief then slumped to the floor in a faint.

Mitch stepped out of the shower and was reaching for a towel when he heard a pounding on the door below.

"Mitch!" Ophelia's voice was frantic. "Come quickly; Rebecca's cut herself. There's blood everywhere."

Wrapping the towel around his waist, he tried to think quickly. Twice during their teenage years, Rebecca had cut herself and fainted dead away. Evidently she couldn't stand the sight of her own blood. He'd often teased her about becoming a surgeon.

"Did she faint?"

"Yes." The teenager's hands were streaked with blood. "I wrapped a cloth around her hand."

"That's good." Mitch smiled reassuringly. "You run back and elevate her hand 'till I get there." He paused. "Where's the new cook?"

Ophelia wrung her hands. "She's delayed. Rebecca's cooking this morning."

"Everything's going to be all right." He spoke clearly and calmly. "You run back and take care of Rebecca. I'll be there in a minute. Oh, and turn off the stove if she's left anything cooking."

"I don't think she'd started cooking yet. Hurry, Mitch." She ran out the door.

Mitch didn't remember pulling on his jeans. Grabbing his first-aid kit from the shop, he raced along the path and took the stairs to the kitchen two at a time.

"Becky." He knelt at her side, brushing the hair back from her face. She was groggy, but conscious.

"Mitch?" Struggling to sit up, she looked at her hand. "I was trying to slice some fruit . . ." She blinked rapidly, trying to hold back tears of pain and frustration. "Can you help me up? The guests will be coming down in a few minutes and I have to make breakfast."

"You'll do no such thing." He scooped her up and held her against his chest. "Ophelia." He tilted his head toward the front of the house. "Can you bring one of those wicker chairs in here? I'd like to make her comfortable."

"Sure." The youngster ran off, secretly delighted to see her boss in Mitch's arms.

"How do you feel, sweetheart?" Mitch gazed down at her, his heartbeat steadying.

"What did you call me?" Her eyes glowed. "Say it again."

"Never mind." He brushed his lips against her forehead. "How do you feel?"

"I feel a little woozy, but you can put me down now." Rebecca frowned. Now why had she said that, when it felt so good to be held by him? She must be losing it.

Ophelia placed the chair beside the desk. "Is this all right?"

"That's great. I'll just check out this hand and bandage it, and then you two can supervise while I make breakfast."

"You're going to make breakfast?" Rebecca and Ophelia spoke in unison.

"Sure." He grinned up at them as he inspected Rebecca's hand. "This isn't too bad, but you won't be able to do much for a few days. Hand me some of that Betadine, Ophelia." His movements were quick and efficient, and Rebecca's finger was bound in no time.

"You're lucky it's your left hand." He placed a towel on the arm of the chair and propped up her elbow. "Hold it up for a few minutes. It's stopped bleeding, but we want to make sure." He stepped back and gazed down at her. "How about a coffee?"

"No thanks, but I'd like a glass of water."

Ophelia raced to bring it to her.

"Well, I certainly need a coffee. Now tell me, what do you girls have planned for breakfast?"

Rebecca glanced at Ophelia, then back at Mitch. "Can you really do it?"

"I can leap tall buildings at a single bound. I can . . ." his voice trailed off as his patient rolled her eyes. "Okay, but I do have hidden talents, you know." He grabbed a chair from the table and straddled it backwards. "When I first went to Toronto I had several jobs before I settled down. One of them was breakfast cook at a greasy spoon on Bloor Street. When it comes to cooking breakfast, I'm your man." He sipped his coffee. "Hey, this is good. Are you sure you don't want some?"

"Maybe in a few minutes."

* * *

"They loved it." Ophelia brought the last of the breakfast dishes into the kitchen. "A couple of people asked about you, but I told them you were busy in the kitchen." She looked from Mitch to Rebecca. "I hope that was okay."

Mitch had moved Rebecca to the kitchen table and forced her to eat a piece of toast and a few forkfuls of scrambled eggs. He grinned up at the teenager.

"You were wonderful, young lady. We made a great team."

Ophelia beamed at the praise, then turned to Rebecca. "I could get a friend of mine to come in and help us for a few hours a day while your hand heals. I mean with the new cook and everything, we might be able to use some extra help for a while."

Rebecca slapped her brow. "I should have thought of that. Go right ahead."

"I'll help you with those dishes and then I'm going to take your boss back to my place for a while to relax." Mitch shot Ophelia a crooked grin. "Come on kiddo, let's get this place cleaned up."

"I was mad at you, you know." Rebecca was comfortably ensconced in a lounge chair on Mitch's small deck. "And the rest of the time, I was worried." She blushed, disconcerted by the way his eyes lingered hungrily on her lips. "But I'm delighted that your wife . . ."

"Ex-wife."

"Sorry; your ex-wife. I'm really pleased she's going to give you more time with Scott."

"It's not definite yet, but my lawyer said it looks good." His gaze skimmed the surface of the lake, coming to rest on the island in the center. "Just think. When he spends the whole summer here I'll finally get to know him. I want him to love the lake the way I do."

Rebecca's heart constricted at his words. She'd worked hard to forget this place. Submersing herself, first in school and then in her career, she had convinced herself that there was nothing to return to. Keeping her visits to her grandmother short, she'd vowed to remain immune to the charms of her childhood home. Yet now, within days of coming back, she had fallen under the magical spell of Muskoka. And Muskoka meant Mitch. The water lapping against the shore, the sighing of the wind in the pines, the distant call of a loon—these formed the soundtrack of the happiest years of her life. It was odd, in a bittersweet sort of way. Mitch was irrevocably tied to the happiest days of her life . . . as well as the saddest. And to listen to him now, he'd be quite content to spend the rest of his life right here.

She studied him as he gazed out over the lake, seeing not the young man of her youth, but the steady, confident man he had become. The girlish dreams and fantasies of her teenage years were nothing when compared with the man who sat beside her now. For the first time in her adult life she didn't want to run from a relationship. The realization shocked her and she shuddered, afraid of what the end of summer would bring.

"You're cold. Are you feeling okay?" He studied her face. "Maybe you should go back and lie down for a while."

"I'm okay. Really." The truth was, she was perfectly content to sit here admiring the scenery . . . including Mitch. What I'd really like is a cup of tea."

"Coming right up."

He was back in a few minutes, a pair of steaming mugs

in one hand. "Just milk, right?" He placed the cup on the low table beside the lounge.

"You remembered." She held the cup clumsily in both hands, eyeing him over the rim.

The words hung between them and a few moments passed before he broke the comfortable silence. "I remember lots of things. As a matter of fact, while I was making breakfast I remembered how you used to love going to those travelling carnivals when they came to town."

She eased back into the lounger, her eyes dreamy and faraway. "And you used to shoot all the ducks and win me a stuffed animal. And I remember cotton candy. It tasted best when they made it right in front of you."

"Would you like to go tonight? I saw them pulling into town when I drove through last night. They're here as part of the summer festival." He leaned forward. "I understand it's excellent therapy for a cut finger."

Rebecca's eyes glowed. "Then by all means."

"I have some business in town this afternoon, and I need to check on a couple of the kids I placed in work experience, but I should be back around seven thirty. How does that sound?"

"Perfect." Rebecca eased herself out of the lounge. "I really should let you get to work. I'll meet you here, okay?"

"You've got it." He lifted her hand, examining the bandage. "How does it feel?"

She swallowed hard. It was difficult to think with him standing so close. "It's fine."

"Don't scare me like that again, huh?" He turned her hand, brushing his lips against her palm. His eyes glittered as they held hers, then slid down to her mouth.

"Rebecca? Are you in there?" Ophelia's voice brought them crashing back to earth. "Lisette's here."

"That's good news." Rebecca wondered briefly if her voice had betrayed her, but Ophelia came bounding onto the deck, unaware of disturbing them.

"She's waiting for you back at the lodge." She glanced worriedly at Rebecca. "You look flushed. I hope you're all right."

"It's the tea." She slid a sideways glance at Mitch. "See you tonight, then."

He raised a hand. "If I'm late, wait for me, okay?"

She nodded and turned to follow Ophelia. The young woman exuded a confidence far beyond her years, and for the first time Rebecca noticed that most of the body ornaments had disappeared.

"I didn't get a chance to thank you properly for taking over this morning." She lengthened her stride to keep up. "Would you be willing to work full time?"

"You mean like a real job?" Ophelia skipped along sideways. "I'd love that."

"Yes. I'd like you to be in charge of the rooms as well as helping with breakfast. We'll sit down later this afternoon and figure it all out. I'll pay you more, of course." She chewed thoughtfully on her bottom lip. "Did you contact your friend?"

"Tracy can start tomorrow. She's been looking for a job." Ophelia clutched Rebecca by the arm. "I won't let you down." She quivered with excitement.

"I know you won't, Ophelia. Gran really knew what she was doing when she hired you." She smiled warmly at the teenager and headed for the office.

Rebecca studied the chart on the kitchen wall. Any of the staff could tell at a glance how many arrivals or departures were scheduled each day. She was pleased to note that most of the guests this month were staying for between 5 and 7 nights. It certainly cut down on the paperwork. She glanced at her watch. Between coordinating with Lisette and Ophelia and ordering supplies, the hours had flown by. Time to get ready for the carnival.

As she brushed her hair, scenes from her past scrolled through her mind like an old film. In every frame, Mitch was by her side, the main character in an ever-changing kaleidoscope of memories. Dragging her thoughts back to the present, she studied the mature face that looked back at her from the mirror. She hadn't expected to see a teenager, but where had the years gone? And what did she have to show for them? She shook her head sadly. A successful career, that was true, but what of her personal life? She'd remained emotionally closed off while life unfolded around her. Well, no more. With a smile, she lifted her chin and tossed her head defiantly. It was time to reclaim her life.

The boathouse loomed silently at the end of the path. The sliding doors along the front were unlocked and she stepped inside, breathing deeply of the sweet smell of freshly sanded wood. Even to her untrained eye, the lines of the boat under construction were sweet. She ran her hand along the hull as she had seen Mitch do, picturing the craft slicing through the clear waters, sleek and powerful.

A goose-necked lamp spilled light over an old wooden desk. She wandered toward the source of light and her eye was drawn to a Homer Winslow print on the wall. She leaned closer. Tucked into the frame was a strip of old images from a photo booth. Her heart stilled. Gazing back at her from the brittle picture, a teenage Rebecca sat on Mitch's knee, arms loosely draped around his neck. In the next picture, she was kissing him on the cheek. In the third frame, they were grinning into the camera, their heads together. She stepped back abruptly, glancing over her shoulder as though afraid of being found out. He had kept them all this time! Lifting them down from the picture frame, she stood staring at them until the images started to blur around the edges.

Something gave way deep inside and tears began streaming down her cheeks, splashing silently onto the desk. The faces in the pictures continued to smile, happily unaware of the changes about to take place in their lives. She wiped her eyes with the back of her hand and peered into the face of the young Mitch, seeing for the first time strength and determination beyond his years. She smiled wryly. He'd been brave to come back to see her, and she pictured him clutching the rose. It had been a sweet gesture by a young man facing an uncertain future, but even now she found herself wishing that he'd made more of an effort to contact her. It had always hurt that he didn't. Her heart swelled as she looked at the picture. At least now she knew that he hadn't forgotten her.

"Becky?" Mitch stood in the doorway, silhouetted in the gathering darkness. "Sorry I'm late." He moved into the room, his eyes darting from the strip of photos in her hand to her red-rimmed eyes. "Are you all right?"

Rebecca held up the pictures mutely. "I can't believe you still have these." A smile lit her face, and she looked down at the pictures. "Look at us. We were so happy."

Mitch walked slowly to her side. "Yes, we were." He tipped up her chin and she swayed slightly, unbalanced by his presence. "Do you still want to go to the carnival?" His eyes probed her face. "You've had a rough day."

"I want to go," she said softly, touched by the concern

in his eyes. "And besides, it's been ages since I've had cotton candy."

Tinny music from the midway blended with the delighted squeals of children as Mitch switched off the motor. The odor of frying onions wafted across the parking lot, and Rebecca realized that she was hungry.

"I will if you will." His eyes challenged her as they stood in front of the Rotary Club's booth, waiting for their hot dogs.

"You'll what?" she challenged.

"Have onions." He grinned. Blinking lights from the surrounding booths danced in his eyes, and she caught her breath, thinking that he had never looked more handsome. "You know-in case you beg me for a goodnight kiss."

"Yeah, right." Rebecca tossed her hair. "In your dreams."

She shoved her hot dog back across the counter. "Onions, please."

Mitch threw back his head and laughed. "That's my girl." He nudged his hot dog beside hers. "Same for me, please."

Rebecca was surprised at how many people came up to greet Mitch as they sat at a long table, eating their hot dogs and drinking coffee.

"You know a lot more people around here than I do," she said a few minutes later, as they waited for her cotton candy. "It's amazing how many know you from your work at the youth center." A new respect crept into her voice.

"That's the nice thing about living in a small town. You get to know people. We help each other out."

Holding her loosely around the waist, he steered her toward a booth, gesturing at the lineup of stuffed animals on the top rail. "What would you like, my dear?"

"Hmmm." She perused the offerings. "I think I'd like that little giraffe. He looks like he needs a home."

Rebecca's gaze did not waver from him as he shot at the moving ducks. His movements were smooth and confident as he dispatched the little ducks with precision.

"Here you are." With a low sweeping bow, Mitch presented her with the giraffe. "And now, would you like to ride the Ferris wheel?"

"Why not?"

"Ladies and gentlemen. Step right up and I'll prove to you that the hand is quicker than the eye." A carny barked his spiel, gathering onlookers around his booth. Mitch maneuvered Rebecca to a space where she could watch and stood protectively behind her.

"I saw this guy last year," he whispered in her ear. "There's no way you can tell where the little ball is." The man moved three little plastic cups in a blur of movement and a young man pointed to the center one, guessing the location of the hidden ball.

Rebecca watched as the process was repeated, mesmerized by the sleight-of-hand. Another man lost his money and went away shaking his head good-naturedly.

"Why do they call it a shell game?" she asked, looking to Mitch for an explanation.

She'd had enough and he guided her away from the crowd. "The first shell games were actually done with a pea and walnut shells. I don't know where it originated, but my guess would be it was a long time ago. It might have been the original deception." He smiled down at her. "I'll be right back."

She stood quietly as he bought the tickets, and they

were soon locked into their seats and swinging up and out over the carnival.

"You're quiet," he said, reaching for her hand. "Is everything all right?"

Her teeth worried her bottom lip and she was silent for a few moments as they rose higher, the carnival sounds fading below them. "I was just thinking about the shell game."

He remained silent.

"I couldn't help but think that much of my life was like that. Nothing was ever as it seemed." She turned and a shadow crossed her eyes. "Do you know what I mean?"

"I think so, but I'd like to hear you put it into words."

She looked at him gratefully. It was important to get this right.

"Well first of all, I knew things were bad for you at home, but I didn't realize how serious it was." She gave her head a quick shake. "I was so naive. And Gran—all her life she regretted not getting the education she wanted. I didn't have a clue that's how she felt." The wheel stopped again and they swayed gently back and forth. "And worst of all I thought you'd deserted me, when in fact you'd come back to explain." Her hands tightened on the safety bar, and her voice carried years of regret as she continued. "I wish I'd known that."

Mitch opened his mouth as if to speak, then pursed his lips, expelling all the air from his lungs. "Me too." She thought she heard a catch in his voice. "Me too."

The wheel started up again and they remained silent for the rest of the ride. As he helped her down, Rebecca glanced toward the parking lot, suddenly tired.

"You've had a long day," he said, guiding her away from the noise and lights. "Shall we go home?"

"Yeah." Slipping on her helmet, she turned to look at

him. "By the way, I still wish I'd been the one to cook breakfast."

"You would have done just fine," he said as she settled behind him, arms around his waist. "You had everything organized. I just applied the heat."

She chuckled and laid her cheek against his back. The bike rumbled into life and they lapsed back into a comfortable silence as they skirted the lake, catching glimpses of moon-spangled water through the trees.

"Thanks, Mitch." Rebecca admired her giraffe. "That was just what I needed tonight." They stood in a pool of light below the back steps. Angled away from the light, his face was partly in the shadows. Reaching out, he lifted her hair from her shoulders, sifting his fingers gently through the tousled strands.

"I want you to know that this is real," he said, his voice low and husky. His fingers tensed in her hair, brushing against the back of her neck. "Whatever was in the past . . . it's gone. No more shell games, okay?"

She nodded wordlessly, not trusting herself to speak. Rising up on her tiptoes, she kissed him lightly then went slowly up the steps, clutching her prize giraffe.

Mitch stepped into the boathouse, his heart still pounding. Wandering through his shop, he intended to check on the canoe Greg had started but was drawn instead to the strip of pictures that lay on the desk. How many times had he looked at those images, wondering if Rebecca hated him or if she even remembered him? His hands clenched at his sides. Had he done the right thing in not telling her about his repeated attempts to contact her? Sitting at the top of the Ferris wheel tonight, with the entire town spread out below them and the lake sparkling in the distance, he'd come so close to blurting out the truth.

Thankfully, his concern for her feelings outweighed the need to exonerate himself. He simply couldn't hurt her by revealing that Stella had screened his calls and withheld his letters. Rebecca was right. Nothing in their young lives had been as it seemed. He tucked the strip of photos back into the picture frame and turned off the light. There was one more thing he had to tell her. Maybe tomorrow.

Chapter 8

Rebecca wandered through the kitchen, checking on the preparations for tomorrow's breakfast. Lisette had everything in hand. Reaching up to turn off the goose-necked lamp, she noticed the two journals under a stack of files and picked them up. She would read them again— perhaps this fall when she had more time. She stopped with one foot on the stairs. Had she really thought that? When had she begun to consider staying here? She didn't know. She waited for the familiar panic, the need to escape, but it didn't come. With a light step and an even lighter heart, she ran up the stairs, heading toward the attic. The journals could wait in the desk until she had time to read them again.

Humming softly to herself, she yanked on the old light cord and crossed directly to the desk. Her fingers went unerringly to the key, and she opened the drawer. She hadn't paid attention to what was in the bottom of the drawer when she removed the journals, and was surprised to see a dark blue box, held together by a faded blue ribbon. Still humming, she lifted it out and slipped off the ribbon.

"Oh no," she said aloud, recognizing her grandmother's writing. "What now?"

Stella's distinctive writing was scrawled across a folded piece of creamy linen writing paper. 'Rebecca' it said.

She lifted it out. Below the note lay a stack of letters. Rebecca frowned, then fanned through the stack. They were all unopened, and all were addressed to her. Every last one was in Mitch's handwriting, from an unfamiliar Toronto address.

She stared down at the letters, her skin prickling with a strange mixture of excitement and dread. This meant . . . she shook her head in disbelief. This meant that Mitch had written to her after all. Her mind raced. What were the dates? She flicked through the stack. They were organized with the earliest one on the top. The postmark was clear. It had been mailed two days after their graduation! She fanned through them. Eight more had been received within the space of a couple of weeks. She studied the date of the last one, trying to imagine what Mitch would have been going through by then. It must have been mailed a few days before he'd come back and encountered Stella.

Why hadn't Mitch told her about writing? And more importantly, why hadn't Gran given them to her? With growing trepidation she picked up the folded sheet of paper, which had fallen to the floor.

Clutching her discovery to her chest, she hurriedly stuffed the journals in the drawer and locked it, returning the key to its hiding place. Suddenly it was imperative to get to the safety of her bedroom.

Sitting cross-legged on her bed, she spread out the letters. Nine in all. She studied them in silence, her thoughts drifting back to the dates on the postmarks. Those days had shaped the balance of her life. And every one had been a lie.

She picked up the first letter, running her fingertips over the address. It was too much to take in.

She didn't want to read Stella's note, but she needed to make sense of all this. Would the note provide it? She took a deep breath. There was only one way to find out.

Dear Rebecca:

You have just left to go back home. Thank you for a wonderful Christmas. I had planned to tell you of my failing heart, but when you announced your intention to come back to visit this coming summer, I couldn't bring myself to do it.

I have kept a terrible secret from you all these years.

How can I explain this to you? When you came to me as a child, I was determined to give you a happy childhood, free from constraint. Hopefully I succeeded.

However, as I watched your growing attachment to Mitch Burton, I became fearful. Having been denied the advantages of an education, I couldn't bear the thought of you marrying too early. By now you've figured out the rest. I bundled you off and never let on that Mitch was trying to contact you.

Sitting here on a sunny January morning I find I can't think of the right words to tell you how much I regret those actions. I see now that I forced you to live my dream instead of your own.

If you're angry, I don't blame you. If you hate me, I can only say that I probably deserve it. But my dear, please know that I truly thought I was doing what was in your best interest.

I love you Rebecca, and I ask your forgiveness.

Gran

Rebecca fell back on her pillows, holding the note to her chest. "Oh Gran," she whispered aloud, "how could I hate you?" Her eyes fell on the letters and in the recesses of her memory the sun came out from behind a cloud. "Especially when you've given me such a gift." Gathering up the envelopes, she placed them in a neat pile on her bedside table. Then she slipped under the covers, eager to read the letters that had waited for her all these years.

"I saw you on the Ferris wheel last night." Ophelia's eyes sparkled. "Greg and I were at the carnival. I called, but you didn't hear me." She sidled closer. "It looked like you were having a good time."

Rebecca grinned. "Yes, we had a good time. What about you?"

Ophelia chatted away, and Rebecca nodded dutifully. She'd been watching out the kitchen window, trying to catch a glimpse of Mitch. Last night, reading between the lines of his letters, she'd glimpsed a young man who'd been forced to grow up in a very short time. His letters had been sweet and heartbreaking at the same time. In the first letter, eager to explain his disappearance, he'd filled her in on the situation at home. That had been difficult to read.

At first he'd been puzzled, asking why she didn't respond. He asked her to forgive him, and to please write back, unaware that by then she was gone. As the days slipped by, the tone of his letters began to change, displaying a fierce determination she didn't know he'd possessed.

". . . but he said he'd find you later." Ophelia's voice trailed off.

"What was that?" Rebecca whirled around. "Sorry, but my mind was somewhere else. What did you say?"

"Mitch was looking for you earlier. He took off on his

bike but he said to tell you he'll be back by noon. Something about taking you out for lunch."

Rebecca's hand flew to her hair, and she glanced at the clock. "I don't suppose he said where?"

"Nope. He said it was going to be a surprise."

"I hope you don't have any plans." Mitch sat astride the Harley at the foot of the stairs, grinning up at her. "I got Midge to make us a picnic."

A shiver of anticipation rippled up her spine. "Sounds like fun."

"Yeah." He lifted his sunglasses, and his eyes held hers for an extra beat. "Bring your swimsuit. We're going to the island."

Rebecca glanced out to the low island sitting in the center of the lake. "But . . ."

"Don't worry. I know the guy who owns it." He rolled toward the boathouse. "See you on the dock in ten minutes."

"I hope I didn't keep you waiting, but I decided to put my favorite canoe in the water." Mitch eased up beside the dock, steadying the canoe with one hand. "Hop in." Rich green trim complemented the distinctive grain of cedar.

"I suppose you made this, too?" She stepped in lightly, settling comfortably in the bow. "It's beautiful."

"Yes, I did." He pushed off from the dock, and with a few deft strokes, he turned the canoe around. "There's a real satisfaction in feeling something come to life under your hands."

She trailed her hand in the water and looked up to see him watching her.

"How does the hand feel today? I brought more bandages in case you decide to go swimming."

"You think of everything." She lay back and regarded

him through half-closed eyes. The paddle cut through the water cleanly, water droplets stringing out like shimmering pearls with each stroke. He switched from one side to the other without missing a beat, and she watched the way his hands skillfully controlled the direction of the canoe with subtle movements of the paddle. The muscles in his arms flexed as the canoe slid silently through the water, and she savored the image of the confident man at the other end of the canoe.

Skirting the shallows on the south end of the island, he pulled the canoe up onto a small beach. Rebecca stepped out, up to her knees in water. The bay was sheltered, the water surprisingly warm. "Do you remember when we were kids?" She stood on the beach, curling her toes in the fine sand. "We dreamed about owning this island one day. If I recall correctly, we were going to build a sprawling house right here." Shading her eyes, she pointed to one of several topless trees. "Look, there's still an osprey nesting here."

"I like to think it's a descendant of the ones we watched." He hauled a picnic basket from the canoe. "Grab that blanket, would you, Becks? We'll sit up there in the shade."

The clearing was carpeted with pine needles and dried leaves. Rebecca closed her eyes, inhaling the sweet, heady scent of pine, redolent in the summer air.

"What do you want to do first?" He eyed her uncertainly. "Eat or swim?"

She remained silent, spreading the blanket on the soft ground. She turned to him, searching his eyes. "I know about the letters, Mitch."

"The letters?" A frown pulled his eyebrows together.

"The ones you wrote to me from Toronto. I found them last night." She waited for his reaction. "I can't tell you how much it means to know that you wrote to me. Nine letters and Gran kept them all."

"Well, I'll be." He walked a few steps to beach and picked up a handful of sand, sifting it from hand to hand. A breeze blew up and the sand drifted away, but he didn't seem to notice. Wiping his hands on his shorts, he moved back into the shade.

"She must have had second thoughts, or she wouldn't have kept them all these years."

"She did. She left me a note."

"And?"

"What do you mean?"

"How do you feel about what she did? Are you angry?" He ducked his head, peering into her eyes.

"Surprisingly, no. I must have used up all my anger a long time ago." She knelt on the blanket and reached for the picnic basket. "And besides, didn't we agree that what's past is past?"

Mitch nodded, his relief evident. He lowered himself to the blanket and sat with arms draped over his knees. "In a way, we were both victims of the same shell game." He reached for two bottles of soda and twisted off the tops. Passing one to her, he held his up for a toast. "Here's to learning what's real," he said, his voice thick with emotion. He sipped slowly, lost in thought. "It boggles the mind, it really does. There I was, a young kid in a strange town wondering why my girlfriend wasn't answering my letters." He grinned crookedly. "And the whole time you were wondering why I wasn't contacting you." He was lost in thought, unaware of the small whitecaps that were starting to form.

"Why didn't you tell me, Mitch?" Her voice was soft, tentative. "I mean now, when I came back. Why didn't you tell me you'd written?"

"I almost did. A couple of times." He ran his finger through the condensation on the side of the bottle, collecting his thoughts. "I just couldn't do that to you. Stella was your only family, and I know how much you loved her. I was afraid you'd hate her or something." His mouth tugged sideways. "Obviously, I didn't give you enough credit."

"A few weeks ago I probably would have reacted differently. But now . . ." A gentle smile lit her face. "As you said, I'm learning what's real." Standing up, she walked the few steps to the sand, deep in thought. She turned, surprised to find him right behind her.

"Are you real, Mitch?" She reached out and touched his face. "Sometimes I'm not sure."

"Oh, I'm real all right." The wind gusted again, lifting her hair from her neck, swirling it around her head. His eyes flared as he brushed it back, long fingers cupping her face.

A ferocious gust of wind shook the trees, sending a shower of leaves and pine needles filtering down through the limbs.

"What the . . ." Mitch ran to the water's edge. The sky had turned dark grey, with menacing clouds scudding in from the west.

The tension in his voice crackled as he hurriedly packed up the hamper. "We've got to get out of here." He kept glancing at the water. "I wish I'd brought the boat instead of the canoe."

"Couldn't we wait here?"

"No." He glanced upward. "These trees are like lightning rods out here in the middle of the lake. Besides, there's no telling how long the storm will last. We should get back to the lodge and make sure everything's okay there."

"Will we be all right in the canoe?" She started to fold the blanket.

He didn't answer her question. "Don't worry about folding it." His voice was tight. "Just get in and grab a paddle."

Rebecca followed orders, and he was right behind her with the picnic hamper.

"I should have been watching," he muttered angrily, "but the forecast was for good weather. Grab that paddle, and let's hope we get home before the worst of it hits."

It took all of Mitch's strength to keep the canoe pointing toward Water Lily Bay. The skies darkened and the wind whipped the lake into a white froth. Rebecca's injured hand throbbed, but she bit her lip and continued paddling. Halfway across the rain started and they both lowered their heads, pulling the broad paddles through the water with all their strength.

"You're doing fine," Mitch shouted from his position in the rear of the boat. "We're almost there." The rain came straight down, huge drops splattering the surface of the lake, drenching them completely.

Ten minutes later, soaked and exhausted, they eased up alongside the dock. Mitch leaned on his paddle, breathing hard. Rebecca stood up unsteadily.

"Boss!" Ophelia ran down the dock, helping Rebecca out of the canoe. "We were watching you. I was so worried."

Rebecca managed a feeble grin. In spite of the fact that they were soaked and out of breath, she had felt safe with Mitch. "We're fine." She shivered. "Just cold and wet."

Greg raced along the path from the boathouse. "I'll give you a hand with that," he shouted through the roar of the storm. Mitch nodded gratefully, and they pulled the canoe up onto the shore.

"You guys go on ahead with the hamper. Greg and I

will be up in a minute." The two men turned the canoe over. "We'll haul up some of that firewood from around back. I think the guests would welcome a fire right about now."

The guests had scurried inside as the first large drops began to fall. Several sat on the screened porch, exclaiming over the force of the downpour, while others gathered around the fireplace, offering advice as Mitch built a roaring fire. Rebecca hurriedly turned on the lights, and soon the room was alive with the crackling of logs and the sweet scent of woodsmoke.

Rebecca wandered into the kitchen and sat down at the table, holding her bandaged hand in her good one.

"Are you all right, Becks?" Mitch came silently up behind her.

She stared at her hand. "I think so, but this really hurts."

Mitch frowned as he saw the red stain and took her hand in his. He unwound the wet bandage, tenderly wiping away the blood. "I'm sorry, sweetheart," he murmured softly. "I forgot about your hand when I asked you to paddle." He brushed his lips lightly over the back of her hand. "I'll rebandage it. Where is the picnic hamper?"

"Right here." Ophelia placed the square basket on the table. "It's sure heavy. Didn't you guys eat yet?"

Mitch applied a fresh bandage and sat back. "No, so why don't we have our picnic right here? I'll put on some coffee. Would you and Greg like to join us?" He started to unpack the hamper. "I think Midge made enough food for an army."

"Sounds good. I'll check on the guests and be right back." Ophelia headed for the great room.

* * *

"That was good." Greg hadn't contributed a lot to the conversation, but Rebecca noticed a growing confidence in the young man.

Mitch gave him a lopsided grin. "It doesn't look like we'll be working any more today, but would you mind checking on the fireplace? Perhaps throw on a few more logs?"

"I'll help in a minute." Ophelia jumped up, clearing away the plates. "Some of the guests have set up a Monopoly game on one of the dining room tables, and the rest are gathered around the fireplace, telling stories about the trips they're planning next." She nodded emphatically. "Stella would have loved this—seeing them all gathered around the fireplace like that." Tears rimmed her eyes, and she gave her head a quick shake. "I'm sorry, Rebecca."

"Don't be silly." Rebecca's own smile was misty as she reached out for the teenager. "I love to hear stories about Gran." She hugged her briefly. "Now you'd better check on your boyfriend before one of the Bledsoe sisters snaps him up." The sisters, aged seventy-six and seventy-eight, were a delightful pair.

Mitch observed the teenager as she hurried from the room. "I can't believe how much she's changed in the past few weeks." He poured coffee in each of their cups. "As far as I know, she worked well for Stella, but she's really blossomed since you gave her more responsibility." His eyes held hers over the rim of his cup. "You're a good woman, Rebecca Lambert. I'm not even sure if you know that."

He set down his coffee cup and reached across the table, gathering her hands into his. "I'm sorry the weather turned on us today." His voice lowered. "I took you out there because I don't want any more secrets between us. I wanted to tell you that I own Osprey Island. I bought it about seven years ago."

"You?" A gust of wind shook the house but her eyes remained riveted on his face. "You own it?"

"Yes." He grinned boyishly. "I always said I would."

Rebecca's brow furrowed. "Did anyone around here know about it? Gran never mentioned that it had changed hands."

"I don't think many people around here even knew it was for sale. It wasn't advertised locally." He drained his coffee. "I'd been working on Bay Street for quite a while and my personal portfolio was doing well. I just happened to pick up a glossy magazine advertising properties in 'cottage country'. Even before I read the description I had a feeling that it was our island. The timing was perfect. I'd just sold a couple of stocks for an enormous profit, and I didn't even think twice. I paid cash for it."

"Wow." She leaned back in her chair. "That's amazing."

Mitch watched her absorb the information.

"Why didn't you ever build on it? Even just a summer place."

A shadow crossed his eyes. "Sharon hated it up here. She said I could go ahead and build whatever I wanted, but she'd never stay in it."

Rebecca winced at the pain in his voice. "What about recently?" She gestured in the direction of the boathouse. "Why would you do all that work on the boathouse when you could have built on the island?"

"I considered it. But the logistics didn't make sense."

"I can see that," she mused. "Hauling everything out there. You're right, it would have been self-defeating."

"Anyway, I doubt that I would have been given a

license to run a business out there. Not that I applied for one, but all things considered, a beautiful home is what it's suited for."

"You're right." She nodded thoughtfully. "Built by someone with very deep pockets."

"It's surprising how many of those people there are. I had an offer just a couple of weeks ago." He shook his head in disbelief. "I know that property values have escalated around here, but the figure he mentioned was almost obscene. When I said no, he told me to keep it in mind. Persistent fellow. He followed it up with an offer in writing that's good for a year."

"Sort of like an ace in the hole." Rebecca swirled the coffee in the bottom of her cup, lost in thought. His revelation didn't surprise her. Even as a teenager, he'd worked hard for what he wanted, and he usually got it. She looked up to see him watching her intently, the expression on his face unfathomable. "Are there any more surprises?" she asked, a half-smile on her lips.

"That's enough for today, don't you think?" The lights dimmed for a moment, and they both looked up as a fresh gust of wind sent pinecones rattling down the roof. "This storm may last for a while, so I'd better go and close the shutters. Maybe you and Ophelia should close all the bedroom windows."

"It's kinda neat the way the bedrooms are all at the back of the house, don't you think?" Ophelia cranked the old-fashioned window and fussed with the curtains. "Stella told me she always thought she'd have lots of kids." They moved to another room. "You know, when I first came here I didn't understand how someone could be so attached to an old building, but now that you're here I see things differently. You're the third generation to live here. That's pretty cool." She shot Rebecca a sly glance. "Maybe your children will grow up here some day."

"Next thing I know, you'll be telling me you believe in fairy tales." Rebecca grinned.

"Of course. And Prince Charming is outside right now, closing the shutters." She ran down the stairs ahead of Rebecca, her delighted laughter a bright spot in the midst of the gathering storm.

"We'd better think about getting these kids home." Mitch and Greg stood in the mudroom, dripping water onto the floor. "Either that, or decide if they're going to stay over." He turned to his apprentice. "You could stay with me at the boathouse. I'll call your foster parents if you like."

"Can I stay too?" Ophelia pleaded, looking at Rebecca. "Would you call my mom?"

"Okay. That way we'll all be here to help if the lights go out." She walked to the phone. "That reminds me, do we have any candles?"

"I know where they are," volunteered Ophelia. "I'll get them right now in case we need them."

The storm continued throughout the evening. Gusts of wind were followed by torrents of rain, but the guests kept busy with games and conversation. Mitch allowed himself to be enticed by the Bledsoe sisters into a checkers tournament and Greg worked quietly on a jigsaw puzzle. Ophelia and Rebecca served hot chocolate with Lisette's oatmeal cookies before the guests turned in, and by ten o'clock they were both exhausted.

"I'll say goodnight now." Mitch turned at the doorway and pointed to two flashlights in the mudroom. "Come and get me if the power goes out." He opened the screen door, holding it firmly against the wind.

Rebecca took comfort from his presence. "Goodnight Mitch." She stepped aside as Greg came through the mudroom and went down the stairs. "See you both in the morning."

His eyes held hers for a moment longer and then he followed Greg, the light from his flashlight marking his progress.

Ophelia rinsed the last of the chocolate mugs and surveyed the kitchen. "We're ready for breakfast. I hope we can sleep with all this wind."

"I doubt it will be a problem for me. I'm beat." Rebecca turned off the light and led the way upstairs.

Mitch reached out to her and she ran toward him, her feet barely touching the ground. Enclosing her in a crushing embrace, he murmured her name, then covered her face with delicate kisses. With a soft sigh, she gave herself up to the pleasure of being in his arms—where she belonged.

A deafening crack of lightning struck somewhere nearby and brilliant light flooded the room. Rebecca clawed her way back to consciousness, the dream forgotten. Something was terribly wrong. The air sizzled with the distinctive, fresh smell of ozone. For the briefest heartbeat there was silence, and then a sound unlike anything she'd ever heard filled the air. The agonizing, tearing sound seemed to go on forever, and she leaped out of bed.

The tree fell as her feet touched the floor. Standing some thirty feet away from the lodge, it crashed diagonally across the building, demolishing the dining room, parts of the great room, and the screened porch.

"No," she cried, throwing open her door. The night-lights in the long hallway glowed dimly, and for a moment she thought she'd dreamt the whole thing. Then a gust of cold air blew up the stairs and a chill that had nothing to do with the temperature wrapped around her heart.

Ophelia came out of her room, eyes wide. "The guests!" She started down the hallway, wrapping her nightgown firmly around her thin waist. "We'd better check on them."

As though bidden, the doors opened one by one.

"Is everyone all right?" Rebecca followed Ophelia as the puzzled seniors squinted at the light. "Is everyone accounted for?"

The guests looked at each other, nodding sleepily. Ruby Bledsoe spoke up. "What happened, dear? I heard a terrible racket a moment ago."

"It's a bit soon to say, but I think one of the trees came down. I heard lightning strike very close by."

"How exciting, but if you'll excuse me, I think I'll return to bed. I expect it will still be there in the morning." The others nodded their agreement, equally unconcerned.

Rebecca watched in amazement as the guests returned to their rooms. Glancing at her watch, she was surprised to see that it was 5:00. Pale light filtered through the curtains. She turned to Ophelia as the last of the doors closed. "I'm quite sure the building's been damaged. I'm going to get dressed and check it out."

The teenager nodded eagerly. "Me too."

Chapter 9

Time seemed to stand still in the aftermath of the storm's fury. Rebecca and Ophelia stopped at the bottom of the stairs, at first unable to comprehend what they were seeing. Pine needles and pinecones were heaped haphazardly against the wall, as though brushed there by a giant broom. They took a few more steps into the great room, or what was left of it. The front of the lodge was missing and as they looked out through the gaping hole, some of the debris shifted, and they jumped back.

"Becky. Ophelia." Mitch's voice was like a part of the dream. "Are you all right? What about the guests?"

Rebecca giggled, and Mitch shot her a puzzled look. "You won't believe it, but they went back to bed." Her shoulders shook. "They just turned around and went back to bed." She reached out a hand to steady herself against the fireplace. "Sorry." She gazed into the sky where the roof had been. "It's a bit much to take in, that's all."

The dust was already starting to settle and her eyes rested on what was left of the old antique sideboard where it lay covered with chunks of powdery plaster. A thick branch stuck out of it at an odd angle, pine needles pointing toward the clearing sky. Most of the dining room floor was missing. What remained was jagged, tilting drunkenly into the basement, which was mostly obscured by the downed tree.

"At least the storm has passed." Mitch's voice was steady and reassuring. Rebecca could almost see his mind churning. "The first thing we have to do is check the power and turn off any damaged circuits." He nodded to Greg, who was hastily tucking his shirt into his jeans. "You can give me a hand."

They disappeared and Rebecca picked up a piece of the jigsaw puzzle, her brow furrowing. "I wonder where this fits," she murmured, studying the piece intently. She looked up at Ophelia and a strangled laugh bubbled up into her throat. "What am I saying?" She tipped her palm and the puzzle piece slid to the floor. She looked around bleakly, trying to focus her thoughts. "It all happened so quickly . . ." Her voice trailed off.

"Mitch will know what to do." Ophelia's confidence was reassuring. "Let's go into the kitchen and I'll make you a cup of tea."

Fighting a strange sense of detachment, Rebecca tried to focus on Ophelia's brisk movements, but she was finding it difficult to concentrate. Scanning the kitchen, her eyes lingered on familiar items, needing the comfort they offered. "There are probably lots of things I should be doing, but right now I can't think straight." She gratefully accepted the mug of tea, cradling it in her hands for warmth.

"I've got good news." Mitch came into the kitchen through the mudroom, Greg close on his heels. "We checked out the electrical panel downstairs, and we only have to shut off one circuit covering the dining room and the great room." He nodded absently as Ophelia placed a mug of tea in front of him. "Fortunately, the rear of the house is on different circuit than the front." He smiled grimly. "At least your guests will have power when they wake up and you'll be able to feed them. Where they'll sit is another story."

Ophelia peered outside, then turned to Rebecca. "It's going to be a nice day, we could feed them some breakfast outside on the picnic tables. They could help themselves." She grinned. "Like a picnic. They'll love it."

"I'll help." Greg turned to Mitch. "Unless you want me to do something else right now."

Mitch glanced at Rebecca and decided to speak for her. "That would be great. Rebecca and I need a moment to decide what we're going to do next."

Rebecca shook off the stupor that seemed to have her in its grip. "Ophelia and I will get dressed and we'll be right back down. Mitch is right. We need a game plan here."

When she came back downstairs, Mitch was standing in what was left of the great room, studying the damage. She walked into his open arms, and his strength flowed into her body. As she rested her head against his chest, feeling the steady rhythm of his heart, she knew that she would find the energy to get through this day.

"I'm sorry," she murmured, pulling herself together with a supreme effort. "I almost lost it a while ago." She turned her head, staring at the devastation that surrounded them. "I didn't realize how much I cared about this old place."

Holding her gently by the shoulders, he looked into her eyes with an intensity that took her breath away. "We'll rebuild. Start thinking about what sort of changes you'd like . . . or not, but we'll have this place up and running again in no time."

They turned together as sunlight spilled over the hills to the east, and Rebecca reluctantly moved away from the warmth of his arms, a determined expression on her face. "I believe you. Now tell me what I should be doing. We've got a lodge to rebuild here."

"You look for the insurance papers while I start making some calls. We're going to need help."

Rebecca stared out over the lake, lost in thought. All traces of the storm had blown over, and the ground steamed from the warmth of the sun. She couldn't recall seeing an insurance file—she hadn't even thought to look for one. The first shiver of apprehension skittered down her spine as she headed for the kitchen office. Within a few minutes she had rechecked every file in the desk. Business licenses, government certification, advertising, building reports—she checked them all. The business files were clearly separate from the day-to-day operational files, but not one of them mentioned insurance. She looked again. Nothing.

The screen door slapped quietly and Rebecca looked up to see Lisette. "Mon Dieu," she said, her eyes wide. "I can hardly believe it. Ophelia showed me the damage from the outside, but she says we have electricity in here." She tied an apron around her waist and stood for a moment, hands on her hips. "If you'll excuse me, I have a picnic breakfast to prepare."

Smiling, Rebecca shook her head, reminding herself how lucky she was to have people like Lisette and Ophelia to support her. She left the Frenchwoman humming to herself and went to find Ophelia and Greg.

The picnic tables had been wiped clean and the three surviving geraniums added a cheerful splash of color. A makeshift serving table with a red-and-white checkered tablecloth stood nearby.

"Hi, boss!" Ophelia's eyes were bright. "Greg and I were just about to start bringing stuff down. This is going to work just fine." She glanced at her watch. "I can't believe it's almost seven o'clock already. Did you see Lisette?"

"Yes I did." She took Ophelia's arm, guiding her gently toward the lake. "You're doing a fantastic job here and I want to thank you now, before things get too crazy."

Ophelia grinned, her youthful enthusiasm bubbling right below the surface. "You're welcome. It's kind of exciting." Her face fell. "Not that it's good, but you know what I mean."

Rebecca nodded. "I know precisely what you mean. Sorta gets the adrenalin going, doesn't it?" She took a deep breath. "Ophelia, did you ever hear Gran say anything about insurance? I can't find anything on insurance for the lodge."

"That doesn't surprise me. Stella had a big fight with the insurance guy. Let me see, was that last year or the year before?" She tapped a finger against her teeth, deep in thought. "No, it was the year before last. She tried to make a claim. I don't even know what it was about, but they refused to pay." She paused, tiny frown lines appearing between her eyes. "What did Stella say? They denied the claim or something like that. Anyway, she was furious." She rolled her eyes. "I heard about that for a while. She said she'd rather go without insurance than pay them good money for nothing. I think she canceled it."

"But when she calmed down, she probably reinstated it." Rebecca's tone was hopeful.

Ophelia shook her head. "I don't know but it wouldn't surprise me if she didn't. She was a stubborn old lady."

Pausing, she shot Rebecca a sideways glance. "I don't mean any disrespect. It's just the way she was."

Rebecca nodded. "Don't I know it."

"Anyway, I was here the day the insurance man came back." She giggled. "She told him to get off her property and stay off." She gestured to Greg, showing him where to place a pile of dishes. "That's about all I remember. Is it serious?"

Rebecca forced a grin. "It could be. But right now you have other things to do. The guests will be coming downstairs soon."

Breakfast was a cheerful affair. Rebecca sat at each table for a few moments, accepting encouragement from the guests.

"But we'd like to stay until next week like we'd planned," said the Bledsoe sisters. "It's such a lovely spot."

"I'm sorry." Rebecca gestured at the gaping hole. "But this is going to turn into a demolition site in a few hours. We couldn't risk having you here."

"You're not going to tear it down, are you?" Don Meldrum slipped a comforting arm around his wife's shoulders. "It's like a second home to us."

"It's a bit early to make any definite decisions, but no matter what, we couldn't take the chance of having any of you on the property. I'm sorry."

"We understand, dear." Elsie Meldrum patted her hand. "But we hope you rebuild, and if you do, we'll be among the first of your guests to return."

Mitch stood at her side, waving as the last of the guests drove away. "All right," he said, rubbing his hands together. "Here's what I've done so far. I have a Dumpster being delivered this afternoon and a crew coming to clean up what we can. A couple of them promised to bring their chainsaws and we'll cut up that tree. Thank goodness it's Saturday."

"Mitch." Rebecca hated to dim his enthusiasm. "I've got some bad news."

"Could it be any worse than this?"

"I'll let you decide about that. How long have we got before your gang shows up?"

He glanced at his watch. "They all promised to be here around one. That gives us roughly an hour. Come on Becks, what could be so bad?"

"Let's grab a coffee and go sit on the dock."

Mitch slumped back in the Adirondack chair and rubbed his hand over his chin, seemingly surprised to find that he hadn't shaved. "Stella, Stella, Stella," he murmured. "What have you done?" His eyes, brilliant blue in the glaring noonday sun, flickered over the lake and came back to rest on Rebecca. "You're sure?"

"Unfortunately, yes." She raked her fingers through her hair. "I'm not sure how Gran could do this but as Ophelia so rightly pointed out, she could be awfully stubborn."

"You'll get no argument from me." Mitch tossed out the remainder of his coffee and stood up, walking to the edge of the dock. A family of mergansers paddled by, the female eyeing him warily. For several moments, he stared in the direction of Osprey Island.

Turning abruptly, his eyes glinted with steely determination. "Okay, here's what we'll do. We'll clean up that tree, as well as whatever rubble isn't salvageable. Come to think of it, I'll need a second Dumpster. Right now we can't determine how much damage has been done to the foundation, if any." He offered her his hand, pulling her to her feet. "While we're doing this, we can think about what we want to do. Like my Uncle Dave used to stay, first things first."

Mitch's friends turned out in full force. Rebecca recognized many of the same people who had stopped by to say hello at the carnival. Exhaust fumes from two chainsaws drifted through the air as the tree was cut into manageable lengths. Rebecca worked steadily, burning small branches in the firepit at the edge of the lake. The sun had slid behind the hills by the time his friends pulled away, their pickup trucks loaded with firewood.

"Where's Ophelia?" she said, suddenly aware that she hadn't seen the teenager for several hours.

"I had Greg take her home after she made the last batch of coffee and sandwiches."

"Good. I'm glad someone is thinking straight." Giddy with exhaustion, she leaned into him and closed her eyes, breathing in the smell of woodsmoke and manly sweat. His steadying presence had helped her through the second worst day in her life. Pulling back, she looked into his eyes.

"What is it partner?" A grin softened the lines of tension around his eyes.

She tilted her head to one side and surveyed the ruined building. "There's nothing like a small disaster to make you think twice about what's important in your life. Too bad it took something like this to make me realize what a big part the lodge played in my life."

He paused for several beats. "Does that mean you're thinking about staying?" His tone was impersonal, as though the response didn't really matter.

She held back tears of frustration. What did she expect from him, after all? Did she want him to beg her to stay?

"I'm thinking about it all the time. I only have a few days left to give them my decision about the new job but I can't seem to make up my mind." She shrugged. "I guess what I meant was that I don't want to let the lodge go without a fight. It's the only real home I've ever known."

A tear slid down her cheek and he brushed it away with the pad of his thumb. Wondering how such strong, competent hands could be so tender, she closed her eyes and pressed the side of her face into his hand.

"Becky—"

She opened her eyes and looked up at him.

"You're exhausted," he said softly. "You need a good night's sleep." His eyes caressed her face.

With a supreme effort, she tore her eyes away. "I know," she murmured. As usual, he was right. She was exhausted, both emotionally and physically.

"I could use a shower myself, and I need to make a few calls." He walked her to the stairs. "See you tomorrow. We'll have coffee together, okay?"

Rebecca awoke slowly the next morning. The song of a warbler pierced the morning quiet and she rolled over, wondering why she was so stiff. Then it all came back. The agonizing sound of the tree splitting and the deafening noise as it hit the house, splintering the dry wood into thousands of brittle pieces.

Padding into the shower, she turned her back to the water, groaning with pleasure as her muscles relaxed. She'd been too tired to bathe the night before. Too tired and too conflicted about the decisions which lay ahead. She shouldn't have given Mitch false hope about repairing the lodge, especially with no insurance and limited funds in the bank. She loved the lodge—that was a given. But she couldn't tie herself to it financially, especially if she decided to return to her former life in Vancouver. Funny, wasn't it—how she thought of it as her former life? She stepped out of the shower, her thoughts in disarray as she toweled off her hair. Did she really want to go back to Vancouver and the daily challenges of her job? Yes . . . and no. Clearing a patch of steam in the mirror, she studied her reflection, as if the solution would be written on her face. With a short, mirthless laugh she turned away. Right now there was no way she could make that decision. Not while the future of the lodge was uncertain. She pulled on her clothes and went downstairs.

"You're awake!" Mitch met her at the bottom of the stairs bearing two mugs of coffee, wide-awake and incredibly handsome. Clean jeans hugged his hips and droplets of water sparkled in his hair. "Here, drink this." He handed her a cup. It was mixed exactly as she liked it and she sipped appreciatively, watching him over the rim of the cup.

"No fair," she murmured. "You're disgustingly cheerful."

He shrugged. "Call me an optimist." He took a few steps toward the gaping hole in the front of the lodge. "Anyway, I have a good feeling about this."

Before she could reply, his friends started arriving. By mid-afternoon they had cleared away all the loose debris, filling two Dumpsters with the demolished portions of the lodge.

"I saw Stu Phillips at church this morning." Brian Henderson removed his gloves, slapping them against his leg. "He said to tell you that he'll be out tomorrow morning to look things over."

Mitch took a deep breath. "I'd hate to have his job. People usually dread a visit from the building inspector, but he was good enough to give Stella an extension on the roof. He wants the electrical service upgraded as well."

"Judging from what we saw down in the basement, that would be a good idea. It's amazing the way they used to wire these old places."

Mitch smiled, extending his hand. "Thanks again, Brian. We couldn't have done it without you." His eyes softened as Rebecca came down the stairs. "Here's the lady of the house."

Rebecca looked around, delighted at what had been accomplished in such a short time. "I'd like to add my thanks. You and the rest of the boys have been such a big help." She extended her hand. "If we rebuild, we're going to have a party and invite you all back."

The mechanic eyed her curiously. "Is there a chance you won't rebuild?"

Rebecca glanced at Mitch and shrugged. "There are so many things up in the air right now . . ."

"I understand." He climbed into his truck. "Well good luck, you two."

Mitch watched as his friend drove off and then turned to survey the lodge. It looked like a child's playhouse, open at the front. Jagged bits of roof hung precariously over the dark gaping hole where the dining room and the great room used to be. Small piles of rubble were all that remained of the shattered roof, walls, and flooring. Both Dumpsters were full and awaiting removal.

Rebecca stood silently, following his gaze. In the space of a couple of days, her life had been turned upside down once again. Strange how life handed out its surprises, both good and bad. She sighed softly.

"It could have been a lot worse, you know," he said philosophically. "We were incredibly lucky that none of the guests were harmed."

"I know. And they were so sweet. Every one of them

wants to come back." The hollow despair that had plagued her since yesterday came back in full force. "I looked again, Mitch," she said, trying to keep the disappointment from turning to bitterness. "I found the insurance file from two years ago. She didn't renew it." She dragged her fingers through her hair, striving for a lighter tone. "It's crunch time."

His stomach growled and they both laughed, grateful for the break in the tension. "Let's take a ride into town and eat at the diner. Midge usually makes pot roast on Sunday."

"Lordy Mitch, what's going on out there?" Midge hustled them to a booth, grabbing the coffeepot along the way. "I hear the place is all smashed up." She peered at Rebecca. "Are you all right, dearie?"

"I'm fine." Rebecca accepted the coffee gratefully. It felt good to be fussed over. "But the lodge took quite a hit."

"So I hear." She turned to Mitch. "Fred and Lionel stopped by yesterday after giving you a hand, and they say it's a wonder nobody was killed."

Mitch nodded. "In that respect, we were lucky."

"From what he said, you should have everything up and running in three, four weeks, tops." Rebecca smiled at Midge's breezy confidence. "Now. You two will be wanting the pot roast, no doubt."

Mitch nodded. "Bring it on, Midge. It looks like we're going to need all our energy in the next few weeks."

Unable to meet his eyes, Rebecca looked out the window, feigning an interest in the passing traffic. How could he be so positive when he knew there was no insurance? Perhaps she should decide now. Get it over with. Surely he wouldn't blame her now if she accepted the new position.

Turning her attention to the hot dinner rolls, she tore off a piece and dipped it into the rich gravy. Perhaps one more day wouldn't hurt, after all.

Stu Phillips clutched his clipboard, shaking his head slowly from side to side. "This is amazing," he said as Rebecca ran down the stairs to greet him. "I don't think I've ever seen anything quite like this."

She glanced over his shoulder, glad to see Mitch coming from the direction of the boathouse.

"Good morning, Stu." Mitch extended his hand. "Thanks for coming out first thing." He gestured to the building. "We've cleared it out so you can check for structural damage. I'll go with you if you don't mind." He glanced at Rebecca. "You can come if you like, but it's not necessary."

"I'll continue with my phone calls." Rebecca had already started contacting every reservation for the next month. Most of them were return guests, and their initial disappointment soon turned to concern for the building. She had just spoken to a woman who urged her to rebuild the lodge just as it had been. If only it were that easy! She went slowly up the stairs. The sooner she got this done, the better. Then she could tackle the truly difficult part— the financial implications of rebuilding.

"Stu will be sending us a written report in a few days, but it's as we thought." Mitch helped himself to a cup of coffee, and Rebecca could almost see the thoughts churning in his head. "He'll need to approve the plans before we proceed." He paused. "If we proceed. The new roof is an obvious necessity, but he will also require us to upgrade the electrical service."

Rebecca tapped her pen on the scratch pad in front of

her. It had taken only a few short columns of figures to confirm what she already knew. Without insurance, they couldn't possibly afford to rebuild the lodge.

"I crunched some numbers." She pursed her lips. "The good news is that there's enough money to pay the property taxes and to pay Ophelia and Lisette for a month. I'd like to do that, if you don't mind." He nodded, and she continued. "After that we have just over twelve thousand dollars."

She blinked rapidly, fighting back tears. "Oh Gran, why did you have to be so stubborn?"

Mitch crossed the room in three strides and pulled her up, gathering her into his arms. She leaned against his chest as he stroked her back, rocking her back and forth.

"Let it out," he whispered, kissing the top of her head. "You've been holding back tears ever since this happened. Maybe a good cry is what you need."

"What good would that do?" She pulled back and looked up at him. "Crying never solved anything." Lower lip trembling, she dissolved against him, her shoulders shaking. "Oh Mitch," she cried as the tears flowed freely. "What are we going to do?"

He held her gently, murmuring into her hair as the scope of the loss finally hit her. Her tears finally subsided and once again she drew strength from the steady beat of his heart. His shirtfront was damp from her tears and she patted it absently as her mind returned to the column of figures.

"I suppose we could borrow money against the property and the business, but that doesn't sit right with me somehow." She paced the floor, thinking aloud. "Gran never had a credit card or borrowed money that I knew of, and she hammered that into me at a young age." She sniffed. "Eventually I couldn't get along without a credit card but I'm one of those rare people who pay the bill the day it arrives."

"That's very admirable, but nobody would own a house today if they didn't borrow money." He watched her carefully.

"You're right. But I bought my condo with cash." She swept her arm toward the lake. "Even you paid cash for the island." She nibbled at her bottom lip.

"What are you thinking about?"

"Huh?" She looked up at him.

"You always bite your bottom lip when you're worried or thinking."

"My thoughts are all bouncing around inside my head right now. I'm thinking that we have to do something. We can't just leave the building with a gaping hole in the roof."

"I've ordered some heavy plastic sheeting. It's being delivered this afternoon."

She nodded. "Good. I should have known you'd have that under control. But . . ." she shrugged, her face reflecting her indecision. "I've had two days to think about it and I still don't know what to do." She stopped pacing in front of him. "What do you think we should do, Mitch? Honestly?"

His jaw tightened. "I love it here and I'd like to see it rebuilt. But you're the one who might go back to Vancouver." A flicker of hope surfaced in his eyes. "Or have you changed your mind?"

She lifted her gaze, trying to probe beyond the chill that slid over his eyes as he watched her struggle for words. "I don't know," she said softly. "I really don't know."

He turned away, making a production of rinsing out his cup in the sink.

"Would you rather I lie about it?" She gripped the back of the chair, willing him to turn around.

His shoulders lifted, and she could tell he was calming himself. "No, Becky. You've never pretended otherwise, but I guess I hoped . . ." His voice trailed off and he gave his head a quick shake. "I did something else without telling you," he said. "I spoke to Bryce Cameron this morning. He's a young builder who's been in town for a few years now. He's going to stop by to look the place over and give us a price on rebuilding."

"But . . ."

He turned and held up his hands. "I know what you're going to say. You don't want him to go to a lot of work for nothing." She nodded. "I've already told him that it might be a waste of his time, but he says he doesn't mind at all. He has a new estimating program that speeds things up and I think he enjoys showing it off."

"Mitch." She took a step toward him and he backed up, the expression on his face more daunting than any physical barrier.

"Listen, Becks. Let's not fight about this." He tried to smile but his eyes were filled with pain. "Right now, I need to get back to the boathouse and supervise Greg. Then I think I'll go out for a while. I'll be back in time to meet with Bryce."

Chapter 10

Rebecca leaned against the frame of the door, watching his broad back disappear down the path to the boathouse. Why hadn't she been firmer? A band of dread tightened around her heart and she turned away with a strangled sob. Torn in several directions at once, she wandered back to the kitchen table and sat down, holding her head in her hands.

Deep inside she'd never stopped loving Mitch, but was that enough? Oddly enough she didn't know. The idea of giving up her independence and making a lasting commitment still terrified her. She moaned softly. When he'd kissed her in the attic, it had been like nothing she'd experienced before. He'd felt it too, she was sure of that and yet neither of them had been ready—or willing—to take the next step. A chilling thought crept into her mind. Was this attraction nothing more than an unfulfilled youthful fantasy? A dream that had lost its spark in the cold light of reality?

Shaking her head, she pressed her fingertips into her eyes. All she could see was the shuttered look, the lack of expression that had transformed his face. And yet . . . in spite of everything, they had never lied to each other, and she wasn't about to start now. She pushed herself up from the table and went to the desk. A dozen more calls to make and the reservations would be all canceled. Running her finger down the list, she sighed and picked up the receiver.

"Hi, boss!" The sound of Ophelia's cheerful voice was a much-needed tonic. Rebecca looked up from the desk with a smile.

"Hi yourself. I was just about to call you." She looked affectionately at the young woman. "You know, I only just noticed that your hair is back to black. At the risk of sounding old fashioned, it looks good."

Ophelia touched her new curls shyly. "Greg likes it this way." She looked pointedly at the reservation ledger in front of Rebecca. "How are people responding?"

"Very well, actually. They all want to be informed when we open again." She shook her head sadly. "I don't even know if that's going to happen, what with no insurance and all . . ." Her voice tapered off.

Ophelia fumbled with the zipper on her backpack. "I brought something to cheer you up." She extracted an oddly shaped package. "It's for the lodge, really." She fidgeted as Rebecca opened it.

"It's a plate." Ophelia blurted, unable to contain her enthusiasm. "That metal thing is so you can hang it on the wall. I got it at a garage sale."

Rebecca felt a lump in her throat. She fought back tears as she examined the old plate.

"Sorry about the chip, but I thought you'd like it anyway."

Rebecca nodded. "You were right. I love it." Delicate sprays of lily of the valley rimmed the border. "Did you know that lily of the valley was Gran's favorite?" Ophelia nodded and Becky turned her attention back to the plate. The words *Home Is Where The Heart Is* flowed in a pleasing script in the center. She ran her fingertips over the hand-painted words and looked up, her eyes brimming. "It's true, isn't it?"

"Yeah." Ophelia spoke softly. "The lodge may look pretty beat up right now, but I just know you'll fix her up again." Her eyes shone as she looked around, and Rebecca could tell that she was seeing beyond the recent devastation. "This place is warm and welcoming, and it has so much character. That's why I always loved working here. I can still hear the voices of the people who come to visit. The way they sit quietly, talking about what they did during the day. Or their laughter when they're outside at night, using the barbeque." She turned aside, suddenly embarrassed. "Do you know what I mean?"

"Yes, I do. When I was young, I couldn't imagine living anywhere else. I thought this was the most perfect spot on earth. Gran started the B&B after I left, but it makes me feel good to know that other people have enjoyed it over the years." She forced what she hoped was a bright smile. "I'm counting on you to help me find a place to hang this, but maybe that should wait for a while." She set the plate on the sideboard. "We haven't talked about your job. Are you willing to wait a few more days while Mitch and I make up our minds what to do? In the meantime, we want to pay you and Lisette for a month." She grinned. "Call it insurance. We'll need you more than ever if we decide to reopen."

"I guess so. But it seems like a waste of money." She brightened. "Hey, maybe you could take my wage and put it into the construction fund, or whatever you call it."

Rebecca shook her head. "You never cease to amaze me."

"Did I say something wrong?"

"Not at all." Rebecca hugged her quickly. "I just feel lucky to know you, that's all." She guided the young woman toward the door. "And now if you don't mind, I need to do some thinking."

"I hope you can think up a way to keep the lodge running. And remember . . ." her eyes sparkled. "The words on that plate can be taken in more ways than one." She ran down the stairs and jumped onto her bike, waving gaily as she pedaled up the driveway.

Rebecca couldn't wait to get to the top of the hill. She grabbed a pair of binoculars and locked the door, laughing at the futility of her actions when the front of the lodge was a gaping hole. Pausing at the top of the steps, she heard a truck rolling down the hill. It came to a stop near the lodge, and she recognized two of the men from the clean-up crew.

"Is Mitch around?" Pete walked to the back of the truck as he spoke. "Steve and I have come to put up the tarp."

"He should be back shortly. Can I help?"

"Nope." He turned to his friend. "We can have this up in no time. I just wanted to let him know we're here." He smiled warmly.

Rebecca waved her binoculars. "I was on my way out for a walk. So if you don't mind, I'll leave you to it." The two men were already hauling the tarp from the back of the truck by the time she reached the trail.

Rebecca settled into her favorite spot on the rock high above the lake, the silence enfolding her like a soothing blanket, a reminder of what she already knew in her heart. She was happy here. She allowed her gaze to drift out over the lake. For the past several years since *Hearts On Fire* had become such a big hit, being happy had rarely entered her mind. There was her work—and more recently—her new condo. The scene played itself out in her memory. She recalled the sense of pride she'd felt when she wrote the check to cover the purchase. At the time, the euphoria of ownership had overshadowed everything else. In retrospect, she felt a pang of sorrow for the woman in the scene, so proud of her accomplishment, and yet—when all the papers were signed, and congratulations offered—alone.

She shook her head. She had accomplished what very few other people had done. She was writing for a hit television series and she was dependent on no one for her emotional well being. She liked it that way . . . didn't she?

Images of Mitch flickered through her mind. She tried to brush them away, but they hovered front and center in her consciousness. Mitch pulling himself out of the lake that first night, the golden hues of the setting sun highlighting the muscles in his arms, his legs, his abdomen. She swallowed hard. On his motorcycle, his back warm and solid beneath her cheek. And his kisses, bringing her more alive than she'd ever been. The memories shimmered through her body, as bright and vivid as the reflection of the sun on the lake.

The truth was, she was a different woman now. She smiled sadly. How could she not be changed, learning the truth about Stella and about Mitch? But it was more than that. It was the sense of belonging, of knowing that others cared. And yes, there was a deep satisfaction in knowing that in some small way she too could nurture talent and abilities, the way she had with Ophelia.

Or had it been the other way around? The bright young woman had an uncanny ability to lift Rebecca's spirits. Like today, with the gift of the plate. Her gaze wandered down toward the lodge. The sentiment inscribed on the plate captured her feelings in one poignant sentence. This was home. She belonged here. She knew it now, and an idea that had begun as a fuzzy, ill-defined thought began to crystallize, pointing the way to a solution to their problems. She stood up, unaware that she was smiling. There was much to be done.

Rebecca hummed to herself as the walked down the trail. This was going to work. Lost in thought, she was startled to hear a vehicle driving up toward the main road. Glancing at her watch, she realized it was later than she thought. A silver van bearing interlocking C's paused by the mailbox before turning toward town. Bryce Cameron hadn't wasted any time, and she was eager to hear what he'd had to say. Dismayed, she saw Mitch pushing off from the dock, one foot firmly planted in the center of the canoe. She stepped into the open and raised her hand, preparing to call to him. Then, thinking better of the idea, she stepped back into the shadows of the trail. He deserved some quiet time as much as she did. He pulled away from the dock with rapid strokes, heading for Osprey Island.

The paddle cut silently through the water, propelling the canoe forward. Mitch's lungs burned from the effort and he trailed the paddle behind him, guiding the direction of the canoe. He willed himself to relax, to feel the smooth wood of the paddle beneath his fingers. A gentle evening breeze skipped across the surface, leaving patches of wavelets in its wake. He drifted peacefully for a moment, simply content to be on the water, then resumed his short voyage at a more normal pace.

At his approach, an osprey lifted off from the nest, powerful wings taking advantage of the air currents. He looked up, and the majestic bird hovered, scanning the water for fish, before gliding away, intent on bringing back a meal for its young. The other adult bird remained in the nest, alert and on guard, keen eyes watching his every movement.

They weren't his birds. He knew that, but he felt a sense of kinship with them that had started long before he bought the island. Those first few years when he'd still been trying to work things out with Sharon, he visited once or twice a year, slipping quietly onto his land from a rented boat. It was the only peace he'd known back then and the island had never lost its magic.

Pulling the canoe up into the small bay, he stepped out onto the sandy beach. Every one of his senses was on alert and he cocked his head as the high, piercing call of the osprey floated across the water. He picked his way along the shore, the tension in his body draining away as the water lapped softly against the rocks. The pine trees smelled sweeter here, the heat of the summer day releasing their perfume into the evening air. Moving inland he paused at the proposed site of the house. In his many sketches, the house flowed with the contours of the land. It would have been nestled in a stand of trees, becoming one with the island. He smiled to himself. It had been a wonderful dream, and if things had worked out differently with Sharon, who knew? He might be living here today.

But this was good-bye. He leaned against a tree, scanning the far shoreline. The lodge was easily identifiable by the bright blue tarp, jarringly out of place between the trees.

Was he being a fool? He didn't think so. The dream of building a house on the island had been wonderful, but he lived in the present. The reality was that they needed money to rebuild the lodge. And he would willingly sell the island to accomplish that. For himself. For Stella. But mostly for Rebecca. If she went back to her life in Vancouver, he would offer to buy the lodge from her. It was his home now and the ideal place for what he hoped would be more time with Scott. He smiled wryly, acknowledging that that wasn't the only reason. When Rebecca came to her senses, she would know where to find him. He'd be here waiting.

He looked around one last time. As an investment, the island had been good to him. Very good. He pushed off from the shore and paddled back toward the lodge. Bryce would bring him a firm price in a day or two, but the ballpark figure he'd quoted for the reconstruction was remarkably close to what he'd estimated. With any luck, the lodge could reopen at the first of next month.

Rebecca sat in an Adirondack chair by the shoreline, a faded quilt tucked around her legs. A chorus of frogs sang lustily in the reeds by the boathouse, competing with the incessant chatter of crickets. Mitch pulled the canoe up onto the shore, unaware that he was being observed. His actions were quick and efficient, and Rebecca watched him longingly as the setting sun highlighted the muscles in his back and shoulders.

"Hi partner." Her stomach fluttered as Mitch turned and peered in her direction. "I was hoping to hear what Bryce had to say about rebuilding."

He crossed the yard in several long strides, and she was relieved to see a flash of white teeth as he smiled at her in the gathering darkness.

"There you are," he said. "I was going to come looking for you."

She tugged at the quilt, oddly nervous in his presence. She was anxious to tell him of her plans, to help ease the pressure he'd been working under ever since the night of the storm. But caution held her back. Her news could wait until everything was definite. She looked up at him expectantly, wondering if the buzzing in her ears was entirely due to the crickets.

He eased into the chair opposite her, combing his fingers through his hair. She caught her breath. She knew how that hair felt and she clenched her fingers beneath the quilt, fighting the impulse to throw herself into his arms.

"Bryce says he'll have his estimate ready in two days." He leaned forward, bracing his elbows on his knees. "I asked him to base his quote on keeping the original design intact. He seemed to understand how we feel about the place." He raised an eyebrow, looking at her speculatively. "We do agree on that, don't we?"

She looked at him sharply. He knew how she felt about the lodge. She nodded silently.

He watched her for a moment, and when he spoke his voice was resigned. "Okay then. The other thing I wanted to tell you is that I'll be gone for a couple of days. I'm going to pick up Scott and take him to camp."

"Oh." Rebecca missed him already. "When are you leaving?"

"First thing in the morning." Standing up, he turned toward the lodge and cupped his ear. "Can you hear it?" he asked.

"What?" She followed his gaze.

"The silence. It's as though the life has gone out of the lodge." His gaze slid down to where she sat huddled in the quilt. "I'd like to hear it come alive again. It needs to be full of happy people and I'd like to make that happen again."

"Me too," she whispered. Should she tell him now? Her eyes studied the familiar face, seeking a clue to his mood but he was closed off, revealing nothing. She longed for a glimpse into the heart of the man she had once known so well. It was torture being so close and yet not being able to touch him, to run her hand along his cheek, or feel his heart pound next to hers. She struggled with the quilt, trying to free her legs.

He pulled her to her feet and she lost her balance, falling against him with a soft cry. Kicking aside the quilt, she looked into his face, thrilled to see a flash of longing that equaled her own.

"Careful, Becks." Strong hands steadied her shoulders, holding her inches away from his body. He brushed the back of his fingers against her cheek—a tender, familiar gesture. His demeanor changed and a soft smile lit his eyes. "You take care of yourself while I'm gone." He slid his hands down her arms until they stood together, their fingertips intertwined.

"I will," she said throatily. He had no idea how empty she would be while he was gone. "Have a good time with Scott."

He nodded. "I will." With a gentle squeeze of her fingers, he turned and walked toward the boathouse.

His figure was barely visible in the fading light as he headed to the boathouse. "I'll miss you," she whispered, her words floating on the night air just as the chorus of frogs stopped abruptly.

Mitch paused, tilting his head at the words spoken softly in the sudden silence. Had she actually said them or had his mind conjured them out of thin air, knowing how badly he wanted to hear her say that very thing? He shrugged and continued walking, recalling his earlier conversation with the man who would soon be the new owner of the island. He could think of no better way to demonstrate his love.

*　　*　　*

"Rebecca, darling! I was just thinking about you this morning."

It was the greeting Rebecca had hoped for, and she smiled. She had forgotten about the realtor's affected manner of speaking. "I called to tell you I'd like to put my condo on the market and . . ."

"Oh, but that's wonderful," the realtor gushed. She lowered her voice confidentially and Rebecca could imagine her looking around furtively. "I'm working with a client who wants something right away and he doesn't seem to care about price. And darling, he prefers your building. Isn't that wonderful?"

Rebecca thought quickly. "I could call the concierge and ask him to give you access. Would that work?"

"You're too clever. Hold on, darling. Do you mind if I buzz my client right now? Then I can give you a precise time." The line went dead and Rebecca leaned back in her chair, watching the antics of the squirrel outside the kitchen window. It leaped from branch to branch, following its favorite route through the trees. The wildlife at her Vancouver condo consisted of noisy, ever-present seagulls.

"Are you still there, my dear?" Cassandra's voice warbled in her ear. "He's absolutely thrilled with the idea and would like to take a look this afternoon, but there is one small catch."

Rebecca suppressed a groan. Ever since she arrived here, there had been one small catch after the other. She should have expected it. "What is it?" she asked cautiously.

"He prefers a furnished place." Her voice lowered again. "It's an Asian gentleman and he wants a pied-a-terre while he's here on business." She paused a moment—no small feat, Rebecca thought wryly. It was no wonder the realtor was so successful, if she moved this swiftly on all her deals.

Rebecca thought of her new furniture. It was elegant, stylish—and cold. Her eyes took in the mismatched set of chairs gathered around the old pine table that had been in the lodge for over fifty years. "I suppose that would be acceptable," she said, trying to control the relief she felt. "Could I ask you to set a price for it? I bought it all within the space of a few days and I recall precisely what I paid for it." She bit her bottom lip. "And if he wants to make me an offer, I suppose you could have someone pack up my clothes and other personal items and ship them to me. I could e-mail you a list."

"Of course, my dear. You leave that all to me. Now let's see . . ." Rebecca heard the rustle of paper in the background. "I'm taking him to view your place at two, and then I have another showing at five, so I won't be able to get back to you until this evening. Give me your number, won't you?"

It had been almost too easy. Giddy with relief, Rebecca wandered toward the dock, a glass of iced tea in her hand. Cassandra had secured an unconditional offer to purchase the condo, furniture included. The sum was enormous, and for a fleeting moment she wondered if she had done the right thing. It had all happened so quickly. She sank down into one of the chairs at the end of the dock, wishing that she could share the news with Mitch. She looked at the lodge and her heart twisted to see the gracious old building shrouded by a tarp. She turned away, picturing it with a new roof; the public rooms lovingly restored to their former glory. Her vision blurred as she recalled the last evening she spent with her grandmother.

As was their custom, they had taken a short walk on the frozen lake, Gran's arm tucked firmly in hers. The ice was over a foot deep and it cracked, the sound echoing like a shot across the snowy, flat expanse. The startling noise no longer frightened her as it had when she was a child, and they stood with their faces to the sky, snowflakes floating down like fairy dust.

Later they had sipped hot chocolate in front of the fire, their voices nostalgic as they recalled shared memories of Rebecca's youth. "This is comfy," she had said, edging closer to the fire. Gran had smiled, her eyes full of love. "When I'm gone," she said, her eyes distant as a burning log settled lower on the glowing coals, "I hope you'll come back often. Maybe you'll even decide to live here."

Rebecca sipped the tea, unsettled by the memory. "I'm doing this for you, Gran," she said, her eyes bright with unshed tears. "But first and foremost, I'm doing it for myself."

Chapter 11

"**H**ello Mitch." Mr. Carmichael stood, extending his hand. He opened a file on his desk. "I see you've been busy." He selected a sheaf of papers. "This is one of the most straightforward real estate transactions I've ever handled. Take your time and glance over the figures. I think you'll find that everything is in order."

Mitch quickly checked the figures and nodded. Bright stick-on arrows pointed to areas requiring his signature and he signed quickly, hesitating momentarily over the last arrow. He'd wondered how it would feel, letting go of a cherished dream, but he felt only a calm determination in knowing that he was doing the right thing. With a small flourish, he signed the last page.

The lawyer separated the stacks of papers, slipping Mitch's copies into a legal envelope. "And this is yours also," he said with a smile, sliding a certified check across the desk.

Mitch picked it up, seeing not the dollar figures, but a refurbished lodge.

"I also have some good news about your son." The

lawyer smiled. "Your ex-wife has agreed to everything you asked for. It looks like you'll be seeing a lot more of Scott in the future."

Mitch swallowed, surprised at the size of the lump in his throat. "That's great," he said huskily. "I'm on my way to see him now."

The lawyer handed over another sheaf of papers. "Congratulations, son." He slapped him on the back. "And good luck."

Scott was full of lively chatter all the way to camp. The clothes from Bermuda were a big hit, and he crammed them into his already full duffel bag. Reluctant to part from him so soon, Mitch watched his son run across the grassy compound, greeting his friends from previous years. Returning to the car, he consoled himself with the thought that in a couple of weeks he'd have the boy for the rest of the summer. He checked his watch. If the traffic cooperated, he should be able to make it back in time for a swim. He couldn't wait to see Rebecca's face when he told her his news.

"Don't tell me you're thinking of giving up everything you've worked for." Rebecca could tell her agent was trying to remain calm. "The suits are starting to get anxious. What am I going to tell them?"

"I haven't said I'm giving it up. All I want is an extension. Tell them I need more time."

"How much more?"

"One week. No, make that two."

"And if they don't agree?"

"I'll still have my old position. That's not such a bad gig, you know. There are other talented writers on the show who can do the job equally as well. They won't be stuck."

"Why do you think they offered you the position of head writer? They want you, Rebecca."

"Well, I'm not sure I want them."

"What's going on out there? I scarcely recognize you any more."

"Oh Leona, I don't recognize myself." Rebecca wandered to the kitchen window, phone in hand. The water lilies had started blooming yesterday, starry pink bursts of color among the waxy green pads. "If I tried to explain I wouldn't know where to start." The lake sparkled enticingly and she felt a sudden need for a swim. "Let's just say that a lot of things have happened, and I need more time to make up my mind."

"So let me get this straight. You want more time to decide about the head writer position, and you also intend to spend your entire hiatus there?"

"That's right." Rebecca was aware she might sound flippant, but she was tired of being pressured.

Her agent decided to give up gracefully. "All right, Rebecca. I'll see what I can do."

"I appreciate that, Leona, I really do, and now I have to run. Talk to you soon."

She changed quickly into her bathing suit, wrapping the pareu from Bermuda around her hips. Had that trip been only a couple of weeks ago? It seemed like another lifetime.

With a running start, she dove cleanly into the water, striking out immediately in a leisurely Australian crawl. Many years ago, she and Mitch had practiced the crawl until their arms flashed in unison. It wasn't until the end of that summer that she realized he'd been holding back to keep pace with her.

She turned around, heading back to the dock. She still swam several nights a week in the pool at her condo in Vancouver, but this was different. This was swimming the way it was meant to be. With a final kick she grabbed the rails of the swim ladder, catching her breath before pulling herself from the water.

Mitch cut his motor and coasted down the hill. The sun shone brassily on the water, almost blinding in its intensity. Time was suspended for a moment as Rebecca stepped onto the dock. She threw back her head, raking her fingers through her hair. It was a familiar gesture from their childhood, and he was glad she couldn't see the yearning on his face. She picked up her towel and dried off, her movements quick and efficient.

Sensing his presence, she stilled. Lowering the towel, she looked directly at him and he had the distinct feeling that she could read his thoughts. She raised her hand in greeting, a smile spreading over her face.

Goosebumps prickled Rebecca's entire body as she patted her face with the towel, and they had nothing to do with being cold. She knew without looking that Mitch was back and watching her. She wanted—no—she needed to be with this friend, this man who knew her better than anyone before or since. But he'd made it clear that he didn't know where their relationship was heading. She gave herself a mental slap. Who was the one who'd talked about returning to Vancouver? She bit her bottom lip. They were both badly scarred, and afraid to commit, but she was confident that for the time being they could work together to restore the lodge. Eager to share her news, she raised her hand in greeting.

His long, muscular legs narrowed the space between

them, and she perched on the arm of a chair, grateful for the support. "I'm glad to have you home," she blurted. *Where had that come from?* "How was your trip?"

He appeared not to notice the blush that crept up her neck. "It was successful." He slipped his hands into his back pockets. "Anything new here?"

"Hmm." She tapped a finger on her lips. "I have some news, but you first. How did it go?"

"Better than I'd hoped. Sharon has agreed to let Scott visit more often."

"Oh Mitch, I'm really happy for you. And he's all settled at camp?"

"He ran off to join his friends without so much as a backward look, but he'll be here soon enough." He wiped his brow again. "Listen, I'd like to get into my shorts. Why don't you come over to the boathouse while I change? We'll find something cool to drink and you can tell me your news."

"It's peaceful over here," she said when he joined her with two glasses. His hair was wet from the shower and he smelled delicious. "I like the way you've left the reeds mostly intact." She indicated a narrow channel leading to his dock. "I used to chase frogs right over there. That was long before I met you, though."

"I'll bet you were cute."

She frowned. "I don't know. But I do know that I had a wonderful childhood here." She watched a bead of condensation run down the side of her glass. "That's why I decided to raise the money to fix the lodge." She eased forward on her chair. "We'll have more than enough to fix it up, I'm quite sure."

"What was that?" He looked at her strangely.

"Well, I'm pretty sure there'll be enough. I don't know

much about renovations, but surely it can't cost more than two hundred thousand?" She could spend that much and still live for years on what was left from the sale of her condo.

He was looking at her oddly. "What's the matter? I thought you'd be pleased."

"I am, I am. It's just that . . ." He shot her a curious look. "Do you mind if I ask where you got the money? Couldn't you have discussed it with me?"

Her eyes snapped. "That's a disgustingly chauvinistic remark." She twitched her shoulders. "I sold my condo in Vancouver. It's far too big for me and I can always get an apartment down on English Bay like everyone else. Besides, I got a pile of money for it. So there."

"Well, aren't we being adult!"

Tears sprang to her eyes and she brushed them away. "Oh Mitch, I wanted you to be pleased. I could see how it was tearing you apart." She took a couple of quick breaths. "Why are we fighting about this anyway? I was hoping we could work together. You know, bringing the lodge back to life, like you said."

"I'm happy, Rebecca." Standing up, he walked to the edge of the small deck, lost in thought.

She waited, more puzzled by the moment.

His head came up and he turned. "Is it a done deal? Can you get out of it?"

"This realtor makes things happen at something approaching light speed. It's signed, sealed, and delivered. I haven't called the bank, but the money is probably sitting in my account right now. But I wouldn't cancel the deal anyway. It feels right and goodness knows we need the money for the renovation."

"With the money we've got right now we could tear it down and build a new lodge."

"What do you mean?"

He started to laugh. "Do you remember when we were young how we could practically read each other's minds? How we thought so much alike?"

"Of course, but what does that have to do with anything?"

"It seems that we still think alike, although recently we haven't been doing so well in the mind-reading department." He sat down in front of her, his knees almost touching hers. "Rebecca, I sold the island so we could rebuild the lodge."

His words took a moment to sink in. "You sold the island? No, Mitch, not the island! It means too much to you. I wish you'd said something."

"Now look who's talking," he chided. "But seriously, Becks, this place means more to me than that piece of real estate. I never would have built out there anyway. It was a wonderful dream, but that's all it ever was. I've learned to be a bit more realistic in my old age." He gave her a lopsided grin. "It saves a lot of heartache."

"I'm all for that," she murmured, thinking that it was probably too late for her. She should be wrapped in his arms right now, but there was no invitation in the steady blue eyes. She looked away, pretending to study the water lilies. He was right to treat her as nothing more than a partner. Until she made up her mind, she had no right to expect him to be anything else.

"So," she said at last, striving for a lighter tone. "It looks like our money problems are solved."

Mitch was eager to share his plans. "I've already given Bryce the go-ahead on the project, so you don't have to make any more of those phone calls. We should be able to reopen at the beginning of next month. Bryce is going to put a full crew on it." He shot her a look. "What is it? You're gnawing on your lip again." He'd much rather be the one gnawing on it, but it didn't seem like the right time to admit that.

"I was thinking."

"Do tell."

"I'm serious, Mitch. Would you mind if I asked Ophelia and Lisette to run the B&B? They're perfectly capable. I'd still sign the checks and do the banking, but I'd like to ease myself away from the day-to-day operations."

Her words chilled him like a cold bucket of water and his jaw tightened. She was already removing herself from the operation of the lodge and that could mean only one thing. "Of course, I don't mind." For an insane moment he wished she'd just leave now. It would be so much easier to get the pain over with all at once. He turned aside. He was overreacting and he knew it but her decision hurt more than he could have imagined.

She leaned forward eagerly. "Do you know when they're starting on the new electrical service?"

"I would imagine that will be one of the first things they do. Why?" His tone was briskly professional.

"'Cause I'd like some heavier power up to the attic. I'm going to clean out a space for myself and put a computer up there. I miss having my own space for writing."

He nodded, not meeting her eyes. "That can be arranged. I'll coordinate it with Bryce tomorrow."

"Mitch says you can start right away." Rebecca signed the contract and handed it back to the contractor. "He says I shouldn't have to cancel any reservations beyond the end of this month."

"That's right." Bryce tucked the forms into a file folder. "As a matter of fact, we should be finished with a few days to spare." He slid the folder into a briefcase on the passenger seat. "And now do you want to show me where you'd like the power in the attic?"

Mitch knew he was behaving like a jerk. He'd been avoiding Rebecca ever since she spoiled his surprise. He chose a new piece of sandpaper, cutting it in half and then folding it carefully in thirds. He'd chosen this task, hoping that the steady, soothing motion of sanding would calm the anger that had been building ever since she made her announcement. He caressed the wood with his left hand, feeling for imperfections as his right hand followed the grain.

She hadn't come right out and said so, but it was clear that she was grooming Ophelia and Lisette to take over the inside duties when she went back to Vancouver. Well, that worked for him! His staff would already be trained when she sold the place to him. He looked around, trying to see the workshop through her eyes and found he couldn't. How had he ever thought that small-town life could compete with the excitement of writing for a television series? One more fantasy shattered.

Fine particles of sawdust danced around his head, illuminated by a sudden shaft of sunlight. He swatted them away. Rebecca was already withdrawing. She was up in the attic right now, tackling years of dust and clearing a space for the computer desk she'd purchased this morning. When she made up her mind she moved quickly, he'd give her that. Grabbing a tack cloth, he wiped away the fine dust particles. The beautiful old wood was ready for the first coat of stain. In his present state, he didn't trust himself to apply it. He would leave that task to Greg.

Massaging the small of his back, he wandered to the open door. Osprey Island crouched low in the water, anchored by fingers of granite that disappeared into the dark water. He tossed down the cloth and took a deep swig from his water bottle. Who was he to sulk because she had spoiled his surprise? What had he expected her to do— throw herself in his arms? He snorted softly. That would have been preferable, but she obviously had other plans. Well, so did he. Bryce was starting work tomorrow, and he planned to work alongside him every step of the way.

He poured the remaining water over his head, shuddering with pleasure as the cool liquid trickled down the back of his neck, soaking into his T-shirt. Just that quickly his anger dissolved, and he recognized it for what it was. Up until now, he'd kidded himself into thinking that Rebecca would once more fall under the spell of Muskoka and stay permanently. He hadn't permitted himself to think beyond that, but he knew he wanted her to stay. With a quick shake of his head he tossed the bottle in the recycling bin. Tomorrow they'd start work on the lodge. Maybe then he'd stop fantasizing about her. Yeah, right.

"It's unbelievable what they've done in only a week!" Ophelia's head swiveled from the lodge to Rebecca and back again. "I mean, it's going to look like it did before, only better."

Rebecca chuckled. "That was our plan. We wanted to maintain the same atmosphere Stella created." She placed her hand lightly on the young woman's arm. "I'm so glad you've decided to take over the daily operations. I know you'll do a wonderful job."

"But you'll still be here, won't you?"

"For the time being, anyway. I enjoy spending time in my little office, out of everybody's way." A shadow flickered across her face. Mitch had been cooperative in their

discussions about the repairs, but there had been no sug-
gestion of warmth, no hint of their former closeness. Over
the last week she had kept to herself, spending most of her
days in the attic. But she could hear his voice, his laughter, and a wave of pure longing swept over her each time
she caught a glimpse of him, tool belt slung about his hips
like a Wild West gunfighter.

"How's Mitch?" Ophelia scanned the property. "I don't
see him around."

"He's fine." Rebecca wasn't ready to discuss the shift
in their relationship. "As a matter of fact I saw him in the
great room this morning installing a new hardwood floor.
You're going to love it."

"Can we go in and have a peek? I'd love to see how the
inside is coming along."

Rebecca hesitated. "I suppose so. Let's go check it
out."

"Greg's supposed to be working with Mitch today,"
Ophelia confided, a blush creeping up her neck. "He says
he learns something new every day."

"I don't doubt that." Rebecca followed her up the stairs.
"Which is it you want to see—the lodge or Greg?"

"Both," she said with a wicked smile. "By the way, are
you and Mitch coming to the dance tomorrow? You've
heard about it, haven't you?"

"I saw something in the local paper, but it's a new event."
She chuckled. "New to me, anyway. Who puts it on?"

"Stella explained it to me last year. Evidently there's
some sort of business improvement association. They're
funded out of the property taxes from all the downtown
businesses and the hotels and B&Bs in the area and they
put on a series of festivals during the year. They're supposed to bring new people into town, but Stella didn't
think they're necessary."

Rebecca nodded thoughtfully. "I'm beginning to understand why she never wanted to go to the Christmas festival."

"Yeah, well anyway this is the summer festival and the dance is part of it. The theme this year is nostalgia." She rolled her eyes. "I'm not old enough for nostalgia!"

Rebecca eyed Ophelia's slender figure. "I'll bet we could find something wonderfully nostalgic for you in the old trunk in the attic."

"Do you think so? That would be great." She hugged Rebecca impulsively. "You're the best. Now let's go and see what the guys are up to. I can't wait to see what they've done with the dining room."

Chapter 12

Ophelia's mouth formed a perfect circle as she stood at the entrance to the great room. "Oh, Rebecca," she said, her eyes wide. "This is beautiful."

Mitch was kneeling on the floor fitting a piece of hardwood. He sat back on his haunches and nodded to Rebecca, then turned his gaze to Ophelia. "What do you think, kiddo? Do you approve?" Rebecca's heart constricted when she heard the warmth in his voice. *How was it possible to miss someone so much when they were right in front of you?* Fighting back tears, she turned to survey the completed work.

Large picture windows had replaced the narrow, old-fashioned ones across the front of the house and cleverly designed folding doors transformed the great room and the newly screened porch into one open area.

Mitch smiled as Ophelia took in every detail. She looked at Rebecca. "It's as though you can reach out and touch the trees." She stepped into the porch. "These new screens are practically invisible. Oh my gosh, the guests are going to love it." She made her way into the dining room, stepping over a package of hardwood. "And these windows . . ." She turned to Rebecca. "We'll never get the guests away from the breakfast table."

Mitch stood up, slipping his hands into his back pockets. "These are all Rebecca's ideas." Something lurked in the depth of his eyes, and her breath stilled. "She seems to know what will work. I wish I did." As he spoke, the mask of indifference slipped from his face.

Ophelia took Greg by the hand. "Come on," she said, "I want to show you what we've done with the rooms." The two young people disappeared, leaving a sudden vacuum.

Mitch stood quietly, eyes fastened on Rebecca. She walked into the new porch and stood looking out at the lake. He came up behind her and his fingers brushed her arm, the first contact they'd had in over a week. In her mind, the clouds parted and sunshine flooded her senses. She was floating, looking down at herself, and her future was so clear she almost shouted with relief. An ache of longing spread through her body and she couldn't deny it any longer. It was so . . . obvious. They belonged together. It was now or never.

"Mitch." She turned slowly. "I've missed you. Can we be friends again?"

"I thought we were friends." He looked at her evenly.

She bristled. "I hardly ever see you anymore." She reached out to touch him but something held her back. Her hand dropped limply by her side.

"What is it you're looking for?" A glimmer of hope flashed across his face. "What do you want?"

"I want . . ." She pulled back, an expression of dismay on her face as Ophelia ran into the room, skidding to a halt.

"Oops. Sorry." Her eyes darted from Rebecca to Mitch. "Hey, are you guys coming to the dance tonight?"

Mitch raised an eyebrow. "There's a dance? Nobody asked me."

"It's a nostalgia dance. Rebecca is going to loan me one of the old dresses in the attic."

"Nostalgia, eh?" He made a show of thinking. "I suppose a person would take an old friend to something like that."

"Exactly."

"In that case," he turned to Rebecca. "Would you care to accompany me to the dance tonight?"

"All right!" Ophelia pumped her fist in the air. "I'll go tell Greg."

"So we're friends again?" Her voice was soft and tentative.

"It's a good start." His eyes glittered like blue sapphires. "I'll see you at seven thirty."

Ophelia fell to her knees in front of the trunk. Pouncing on a flamboyant purple dress with saucy fringes she walked to the mirror. "May I borrow this one?" she asked, her expression bordering on reverence. "It's the most beautiful thing I've ever seen."

"Of course you may." Rebecca stood behind her, smiling at the young woman's reflection in the mirror. "It suits you perfectly."

Ophelia hugged her gratefully. "And Mitch won't be able to resist you in your graduation dress."

"We'll see about that." *Was it too much to hope for?* She ran her fingers through her hair. "I'm going into town to that drop-in hairdresser. I think I deserve a little spoiling."

An hour and a half later, Rebecca drove back to the lodge. The workmen had left for the day, and the somnolent heat of the late afternoon lay over the lake like a mirage. Gripped by a sense of purpose, she checked her watch. It was three hours earlier in Vancouver; the perfect time to call her agent and inform her that she wouldn't be coming back. She ran lightly up the stairs and picked up the phone.

Mitch held the phone in a crushing grip. "He was unconscious when you found him?" He could hear his voice rising. "But he's conscious now and the doctor's with him? How could this have happened?" His heart was beating wildly as he imagined the worst. He stared out at the lake without seeing anything. "Of course I'm upset. He's my son." He bowed his head, listening to the camp director. "All right, but I'm on my way. Please tell him that." He checked his watch impatiently. "I don't know. A couple of hours, I think." He nodded. "Yes, I'll be careful."

He gunned the motor and skirted the lake in record time, en route to the highway. "Please God," he prayed through clenched teeth. "Don't let anything happen to him." The onramp to the highway came as a surprise. He hadn't even been aware of driving through town. He took a few deep, calming breaths and merged into traffic.

The information had been sketchy. Scott had fallen from a tree. Another camper was involved, but the details weren't clear. A clutch of fear gripped him and he forced himself to relax his hold on the steering wheel. Thankfully, the camp hadn't been able to contact Sharon. It was selfish, he knew, but he didn't think he could handle her dramatics right now. He hated to admit it, but he was frightened enough for both of them. His thoughts raced, dredging up every scrap of info he could remember about head injuries. The lasting effects could be devastating and he fought the urge to speed up again. He concentrated on reliving treasured moments of his time with Scott.

He pulled up at the camp's administration building as the campers poured out of the mess tent, preparing for their evening activities.

"Mr. Burton?" The doctor must have been waiting for him. "I'm Dale Meadows, the camp physician and swimming instructor. Come this way, please. Scott is awake now and looking forward to seeing you."

"Hi, Dad." Scott was sitting up in bed, one arm in a cast and a sheepish smile on his face. Mitch noted with interest that every speck of food on his meal tray had been cleaned up. Relief swept through him.

"It turns out that your son is quite the hero." The doctor smiled down at Scott. "Show your dad the bump on your head, son."

Mitch walked to the opposite side of the bed. He wanted to pull Scott close, but several other youngsters were in the tent and he restrained himself, not wanting to embarrass his son. He contented himself with a gentle squeeze on the boy's shoulder. "That's going to be a dandy lump." He examined the cast. "So what's this about being a hero?"

Scott looked up, his young face earnest. "I don't think I'm a hero, Dad. But when I saw how frightened Eric was way up there in that tree, I thought somebody better help him down."

"One of the younger campers," explained the doctor. "He could have been seriously injured if Scott hadn't helped him down."

"Yeah." Scott grimaced. "But then I fell myself." He gingerly touched his head. "Some rescue."

"Well, I'm here to take you home, son. You can recuperate with me at the lake."

Scott's face fell. "But Dad." His gaze flickered between his dad and the doctor. "I was hoping to stay." He waved the cast. "It's only my left arm. And the kids all want to sign my cast."

The young doctor looked at Mitch. "Your dad and I will be right back," he said, guiding Mitch from the tent.

"I know how you must feel and of course we'll respect your wishes," he said thoughtfully, "but I can't see the harm in it. His arm has only a hairline fracture, and there is no sign of a concussion." He shot Mitch a bemused glance. "Besides, what kid wouldn't enjoy a bit of adulation from his peers?"

"I suppose you're right, but if you don't mind I'll stick around for a while and reassure myself." He extended his hand. "Thanks for everything. You'll keep an eye on him, won't you?"

"You can count on it."

"Come on, Dad. We can take a walk down by the lake." The youngster cradled his cast in a sling. He already had a good start on his collection of autographs. Pausing by the canoes, he looked up at his father. "Dad," he began tentatively. "I was wondering. Do you think you're ever going to get married again?" His blue eyes were clear and steady. "Mom has a new boyfriend, and she says he makes her happy." He peered up at his father. "I want you to be happy, too."

Mitch touched the boy's head tenderly, avoiding the lump. "What brought this on?"

"I dunno." Scott's eyes darted back to the camp. "A lot of the guys have divorced parents. They say their dads are happier when they get married again."

"I'm happy, son. I have my boats, and I have you." A picture of Rebecca flashed before his eyes and the color drained from his face. The dance! He had forgotten all about it! "Listen, Scott. Speaking of ladies, I just remembered I promised to take an old friend to a dance tonight. I'm going to be late, but I'd better get back there and apologize."

"Why don't you phone her?"

Mitch paused, then shook his head. "No, son. This is something I have to do in person."

"Yeah." The boy nodded sagely. "Girls hate it when you're late."

A glance at his watch told him that the time was 9:15 as he approached the turnoff. He hesitated only a moment and then turned onto the little-used Old Lake Road. It skirted the town and should be a few minutes quicker at this time of night. He worked his jaw, trying to relieve the tension that had built up over the interminable drive home. How could he have done this to her again? Soft yellow lights spilled from the windows of the summer cottages along the shore but he barely noticed them in his haste to get back to the lodge. Please! Let her be there.

Rebecca had a sudden sense of déjà vu as she brushed her hair. The brush stilled as a prickling sensation danced along her arms. The hazel eyes in the mirror were unchanged since her teenage years, but tonight they glowed. She had finally decided to take the final step in reclaiming her life. Picking up her lipstick, she leaned closer to the mirror, applying the rich red color with a few deft strokes.

Her hand trembled slightly as she put the lipstick away, and the small stone in the ring on her finger caught the light. Call it sentimental. Call it a foolish attempt to erase the old memories, the old pain. Tonight, as the saying went, she was starting the rest of her life.

She looked again at her reflection in the mirror. She looked happy for the first time in ages. Was it any wonder? Tonight she was going to tell Mitch that she was staying, that she loved him. The clock in the downstairs hall chimed softly. 7:30. She flicked off the lights and smiled into the darkened room. Tonight she hoped to write a happy ending . . . and perhaps a new beginning.

Rebecca stole another look at her watch. 8:17. Four minutes later than the last time she looked. At first she'd waited impatiently in the lodge. Then a quick check of the boathouse showed it to be deserted and she slumped into one of Mitch's deck chairs, her earlier euphoria draining away, her confidence shattered. How could he do this to her again? Recalling a similar night eleven years ago, she pressed her fingers to her temples, trying to block out the painful memories.

A loon called somewhere down the lake and a few moments later its mate responded, the haunting call floating over the water. How many times had she and Mitch listened to those calls? What did he used to say about the loons? She sat up abruptly as the memories came flooding back. Every time they called he reminded her that like the loons, he'd always come back to her. And then he'd disappeared.

She took off the ring and held it up to the light. But he hadn't really disappeared. She knew that now. He'd been true to his word and come back for her. In a matter of moments, despair gave way to apprehension. Mitch wouldn't leave her again. She knew it as surely as she knew her own name. Berating herself for losing time on self-pity she jumped up and checked the apartment for clues, but there was nothing to indicate where he'd gone. She looked outside. He'd taken his motorcycle, and her mind raced ahead. What if he'd had an accident? It was possible. People had motorcycle accidents every day.

"Not now!" she said aloud. "Not when I've finally figured everything out."

She ran for her purse, fumbling inside for her car keys. "Calm down," said a voice in her head. "You're getting ahead of yourself."

Her hand was trembling so violently that she couldn't get the key in the ignition. She slumped back against the seat. "You're right," she replied to the voice. "I'm no good to him like this."

She gripped the steering wheel and stared straight ahead, forcing herself to take several deep breaths. "All right," she said, sliding the key into the ignition. "That's better."

She pulled up in front of the emergency entrance at the hospital. The waiting room was empty and the admitting nurse greeted her with a smile. "May I help you?"

"Have there been any emergencies? This afternoon or this evening?" She gripped the counter, praying for good news.

"No. It's been really quiet today." The nurse gave a quick shake of her head. "Have you checked with the OPP?"

The Ontario Provincial Police told her the same thing. No accidents. No emergencies. "Everybody's at the festival, I guess. I hope it stays like this all night." The burly officer leaned on the desk. "Anything else I can do for you?"

Rebecca backed away. "No thanks."

She crossed the parking lot to her car. She was still worried. She'd go home and wait.

Her stomach growled as she drove past the diner. On impulse, she parked in the empty lot and went inside.

"Hello, dearie. I hear the lodge is coming along just fine." Midge greeted her warmly. "What can I get you?"

"I don't know." Rebecca's head felt fuzzy. "I haven't eaten for a while but I couldn't handle a meal right now." She read the daily specials. "How about a cup of coffee and a piece of banana cream pie." She slid onto a stool.

Midge served the pie and coffee then wiped the spotless counter, watching Rebecca out of the corner of her eye. "I saw Mitch earlier. He sure must have been in a hurry to get somewhere. I've never known him to drive by without waving. Is everything okay?"

Rebecca's hand stilled, a forkful of pie halfway to her mouth. "I don't know," she said, suddenly alert. "What time was that?"

"Let's see. I mentioned it to Reg Bowman, so it must have been about five thirty." She tapped her watch. "You can set your watch by Reg."

Rebecca frowned at the pie and pushed it aside. "Sorry, Midge. I guess I'm not hungry. To tell the truth, I'm worried. Mitch and I had planned to go to the dance tonight, but he didn't show up."

"Oh, hon." Midge moved her bulk to the stool beside Rebecca. "If he didn't show up it must be something serious. Anyone can see that boy loves you like crazy."

"Do you really think so?" She looked down at the ring, but it wasn't there. She must have left it at Mitch's place.

Midge planted a hand on her hip. "Anyone who's not blind can see it. Besides, he's never brought a woman in here before you." She nodded firmly. "So there." She bustled back behind the counter. "So where are you off to then?"

Rebecca forced a laugh. "I don't know. I've been running around in circles looking for him."

"You go on home now. He'll be home soon enough."

"I hope you're right." Rebecca took a sip of coffee them slid off the stool, setting some money on the counter. "Thank you, Midge. For everything."

The other woman grinned. "Get along with you. And give him my love."

Rebecca's heart was in her mouth as she turned off the motor and coasted down the hill. Dim lights filtered through the trees. Mitch had returned.

She felt her way along the path, her footsteps muffled by the layer of pine needles.

Mitch was slumped in one of the deck chairs, long legs stretched out before him. Light from inside the boathouse illuminated the side of his face, and she stood for a moment, taking in the familiar planes of his face. Her heart beat wildly as she spoke his name.

His head swiveled slowly, eyes glittering in the dim light. He rose with one long, graceful movement and stood before her, searching her face.

He opened his hand. In his palm, the ring appeared small and delicate. His eyes moved from the ring to her face. "You kept it all these years," he said, a faint smile lighting his face from within.

She nodded, unable to speak.

He reached out tentatively, touching her cheek. She closed her eyes and leaned into his hand. "Rebecca," he murmured, "I'm so sorry about tonight. About everything."

She gazed up into the eyes she loved so well. "Don't be sorry. I was worried about you." She dropped her eyes. "Well, at first it seemed like our graduation night all over again but then I remembered the loons."

"The loons?" He looked out over the moon-spangled

lake then nodded in comprehension. "I'd almost forgotten. I always told you I'd come back for you." He tipped up her chin. "And I did."

"What happened? Where did you go?"

"I had to go to Scott. He broke his arm." She gasped, and he shook his head. "He's fine. A broken arm that will heal quickly and a bump on his head. He's loving the attention." He took her hand and lifted it to his mouth. "But driving back here tonight . . . well, I had a lot of time to think. I thought about what you mean to me and how I've been afraid to tell you." He grinned sheepishly. "It's time I swallowed my pride and told you how I really feel. I love you, Becky. I love you so much it's making me crazy. Please stay."

She placed a hand on his chest. "Say it again. Those are the sweetest words in the world."

"I love you, Becks, and I want you to stay."

She let out a long, contented sigh. "And I love you, Mitch. She snuggled up against his broad chest. "I've never stopped loving you. I phoned my agent today. I'm not going back."

He backed up and shook his head, clearly puzzled. "That's wonderful but what about Ophelia and Lisette? I thought you were training them to take over."

"I am. That leaves me more time to write." She grinned. "Up in the attic." She trailed her fingers over his face, needing to touch him. "I never want to be too far away from you again."

"Nor I you," he said simply, fingers combing gently through her hair. The tenderness in his eyes was sweet confirmation of his words. A soft moan escaped her lips as he brought his mouth down, kissing her hungrily. She was vaguely aware of the sound of water lapping against the shore as his mouth slanted over hers, sending her into a spiraling free-fall of sensation.

"About that dance," he murmured, lifting his head. "Do you still want to go?"

"What dance?" Her eyes sparkled. "If you think I'm going to share you tonight, you're crazy."

"I was hoping you'd say that." He wrapped his arms around her and they stood on the deck, listening to the night sounds and the beating of each other's hearts.

She leaned back and for a moment she took pleasure in looking at him. Why had it taken her so long to realize that he was everything she'd ever wanted in a man— maybe even more?

"I love you, sweetheart," he said, his voice jagged with emotion. "Do you know how good that sounds?"

"It sounds wonderful. I'll never get tired of hearing you say it. I love you, too."

"In that case, there's only one thing left to say."

"Oh?" Her voice grew softer. "What's that?"

"Will you marry me?" He held up the ring. It glowed softly in the moonlight and together they slipped it back on her hand where it belonged.

For the briefest moment she thought she smelled lily of the valley.

"I thought you'd never ask." She had come home.